Annie Dunne

Annie Dunne

Sebastian Barry

Thorndike Press • Chivers Press
Waterville, Maine USA Bath, England

This Large Print edition is published by Thorndike Press, USA and by Chivers Press, England.

Published in 2002 in the U.S. by arrangement with Viking Penguin, a member of Penguin Putnam Inc.

Published in 2002 in the U.K. by arrangement with Faber and Faber Limited.

U.S. Hardcover 0-7862-4592-1 (Basic Series)
U.K. Hardcover 0-7540-7460-9 (Chivers Large Print)
U.K. Softcover 0-7540-7461-7 (Camden Large Print)

The text of this Large Print edition is unabridged.
Other aspects of the book may vary from the original edition.

Set in 16 pt. Plantin by Myrna S. Raven.

Printed in the United States on permanent paper.

British Library Cataloguing in Publication Data available

ISBN 0-7862-4592-1 (lg. print : hc : alk. paper)

To Derek Johns

Chapter One

Oh, Kelsha is a distant place, over the mountains from everywhere. You go over the mountains to get there, and eventually, through dreams.

I can picture the two children in their coats arriving. It is the start of the summer and all the customs of winter and spring are behind us. Not that those customs are tended to now, much.

My grand-nephew and grand-niece, titles that sound like the children of a Russian tsar.

My crab-apple tree seems to watch over their coming, like a poor man forever waiting for alms with cap in hand. There is a soughing in the beech trees and the ash, and the small music of the hens. Shep prances about like a child at a dance with his extra coat of bog muck and the yellow effluents that leak into yards where dogs like to lie.

The children's coats are very nice coats, city coats. Their mother does not neglect the matter of coats, whatever else I could say about her. But they are too nice for a farmyard existence. We will wrap them in old brown paper and put them in the small blue cupboard in their room, and keep the moths from them as best we can.

I herd the children like little calves through the lower leaf of the half-door and into the beautiful glooms of the kitchen. The big sandwiches lie on the scrubbed table, poised like buckled planks on blue and white plates. Words are spoken and I sense the great respect Sarah has for their father Trevor, my fine nephew, magnificent in his Bohemian green suit, his odd, English-sounding name, his big red beard and his sleeked black hair like a Parisian intellectual, good-looking, with deep brown angry eyes. He is handing her some notes of money, to help us bring the children through the summer. I am proud of her regard for him and proud of him, because in the old days of my sister's madness I reared him. My poor sister Maud, that in the end could do little but gabble nonsense.

The great enterprise now, with Trevor and the children's mother, is to cross the sea to London and see what can be done. There are only stagnant pools of things to tempt him here in his own country, there is nothing. He has trained himself up by a scholarship and I can smell the smell of hope in him, the young man's coat. But his hope is proficient and true. I have no doubt but that he will find himself and his care a place to lodge, and fetch about him, and gain employment. He has his grandfather's wholeness of purpose, who rose from a common police recruit to be the chief superintendent of B Division in Dublin, the capital of the whole country.

His father, Matt, Maud's husband, who as good as threw me from the house when finally she died, may drag his polished boots every morning from that rented house in Donnybrook to the savage margins of Ringsend, where he teaches painting and drawing to children who would as much like to learn them as to eat earwigs. Back and forth on that black bike with its winter lamp and ineffectual bell, thinking only of the summer when he can paint the midgy beauties of Wicklow, cursing his fate.

But Trevor has the strength and purpose of another generation, with his red beard.

He is kissing the children's heads now and saying goodbye, be good, see you in a few months.

'Every day I will write to you,' says the

little boy, which is comical since he is too young to know his writing. But the father is not listening to the son, he is staring away into nowhere, distracted no doubt by all the things he has to do, the arrangements, the tickets, the prayers that I think will rise up unbidden, though I know he professes to be a Godless man, one of those modern types that would make me fearful if it was not him.

'Every day, every day,' says the boy emphatically.

'I am going to press flowers for you all summer in my autograph album,' says the little girl. 'There won't be anyone to write their names in it down here.'

'Look after yourselves in London,' I say to him. 'And you need not for a moment worry about the children. You will have enough to do setting yourselves up.'

'As soon as everything's in place, we'll send for them,' Trevor says. 'Thank you, Aunty Annie. It's an enormous help.'

'It's no trouble, God knows. We are lucky to have them.'

'Don't spoil them,' he says.

'We will not. But we will look after them, certainly.'

'Good,' Trevor says, and kisses my cheek, and away with him out into the paltry sunlight. He doesn't look back, though the children rush to the door.

'Come in now,' I say, in case they are going to miss their father loudly, like the knobs on a wireless suddenly turned up, 'and we'll show you your beds, and you can put your bits and bobs in the drawers and we'll be shipshape.'

We hear, all of us, Sarah and me and the little ones, the car reversing out of the rough yard and out again onto the green road to Kiltegan. He will not go home by the Glen of Imail because he fears the rutted tracks and rightly. Oh, it is some other, older year still in those lonesome districts, no calendar there says 1959.

'Sarah and me scrubbed out the old room,' I say gently.

For a moment they are stuck, like beasts in the gap between two fields.

'When you're not here with us, this old room goes to cobwebs. Though it got a mighty spring clean with the rest of the premises just in April. I limed the walls, so don't lean your nice clothes on them, or you'll be getting streaks. And the fire is lit these two days, and the mattresses are aired as you'd like.'

The room is bleak, the room is bare. A tiny hill of brown turf with seams of garnet fire steams in the grate. The window is as small as an owl and frames the lower clutter of the ash tree outside, the big fierce hair of thin branches that grows up from the root.

The fireplace is a hole with a thin strip of painted iron for a mantelpiece. Nothing ticks in that room, the big clock is in the kitchen.

'Are the mice still above us, Auntie Anne?' the boy asks, and I can sense him make the leap, the little leap to us. He calls me Auntie Anne like his father, I notice, though in truth I am his great-aunt. It is like a compliment.

'The mice?' I say absently, inserting their small supply of clothes into the drawers smelling of mothballs and the dry, small bones of herbs in a tight net. I feel relief like a luxury, like a strip of chocolate. 'This house was never without mice.

'Now,' I say, when the clothes are nestled in properly, 'you're Wicklow people now. And this is your nest. And it's nice to have nestlings again in the nest. I hope you won't put too great a strain on old bones! Come back out to the kitchen and eat.'

They don't know anything about old bones. They follow me into the kitchen du-tifully. All of the world is new, and very little, if any of it, is ugly to them. Nothing is old. They do not know anything about the exhaustion of minding children.

Towards the end of the day these times I go slower and slower, like a bad clock. My movements lessen and I reach across gaps with parsimonious expense of energy. Even my words stretch longer. I feel a sudden fear that we are too old to guard these little ones. A hundred tasks and now, two creatures as vigorous as steam engines.

But the fear passes and my sense is only of the deepest pleasure, the deepest anticipation. Two small children in a small country kitchen, wolfing the enormous sandwiches. The flagstones underfoot polished to an impressive green darkness. The dresser against the wall beside the door to my and Sarah's bedroom, which looms at your back when you sit by the fire. All the pride of our delf is there, simple objects enough, the chipped items retired to the topmost shelf. Long strips of notched wood hold the plates from falling. There are but two books there, both thick and wrapped in dark brown paper — my father's family Bible and his complete works of William Shakespeare, side by side like a set of twins.

The lights in the room are always evening lights.

13

These are important matters.

'I was afraid of the sandwiches,' says the boy, eating fiercely.

'Why?'

'Because of your butter.'

'Well, there is no butter on them,' I say, tenderly. I would not take offence at a little boy. We were careful, Sarah and I, not to put butter on the bread. Our country butter has no salt and the children will need a few days to get used to it. We were fearful they would reject the sandwiches and all the work that went into them.

Sarah seems to loom a little, up the top of the kitchen in the shadows, and there are many shadows. She is like a person not used to houses, strangely, but a creature from out of doors, a hare, a bittern. But her face is smiling, beaming, she keeps turning her head like a lighthouse engine, and shines her yellow smile down on the children.

Her head is a mass of powdery white hair, whereas mine is a mute grey, and she smells of something, not unpleasant but difficult to identify, not sweet or perfumed. It may be the starch in her blouses under the forgiving blue and white overdress, it may be the very starched nature of her own skin, kept scrubbed and soaped by means of a daily wash-down at her jug and basin in the bedroom.

There is nothing in the house that we have not scrubbed.

She is not beautiful in any accepted book of beauty, but she is appealing, covetable. She is also thin and so seems tall, like many of her family, and to the children she must seem almost endless, she goes up and up and only ends in the clouds of her hair. Her mother and my mother were sisters, but I do not think a stranger would see a resemblance.

For seven generations my family were the stewards on the Humewood estate, and hers were the coppicers, when coppicing was still a trade. If wooden staves from foreign parts had not become the fashion, the hazel woods so combed and cut by Sarah's grandsires might still be scenes of dexterity and expertise. And but that my father was not inclined to the land, he might have followed a similar course, and never left these districts — and saved himself a lot of trouble later. Such things bind us, Sarah and me, though more truly it was necessities, economies, that carried me back here to her. I was happy with my lot in Dublin, with Maud and Matt, rearing the three boys, but that's all history now. Time runs on and has no width. Those small boys are men, and Maud is dead.

Oh, we are blessed in the company of these children. It is our chance. It isn't that we don't know it. A glee suffuses us, like beaten egg whites folded into sugar.

When the children are fed I bring them over to the wall, the blind wall of the alcove one side of the fire, where the hag's bed should be, except there is no hag now to sleep there.

Properly speaking the hag was the old mother of the house, who would give up her room and her marriage bed when her son wed, and brought a fresh bride into the house. I suppose Sarah and me are the hags now. Neither of us ever had the luck to be mothers, though. When we were young women we wanted to be.

It is there in the alcove, as small as any hermit's cell, where once a bed of branches and straw abided, that we have measured the children over the few years of their lives, when we have had our chance at them.

The little boy is four, and when I press him against the damp plaster I see there has been no great leap of height in the intervening year.

The girl, now six and a bit, has sprung up by three inches and more.

The boy's hair is black as a blackbird and it rests against the plaster like a smudge of soot. He is placid and willing, and stands there like a little sentry, smiling. I am afraid in my heart I believe a boy is worth two girls but I cannot help that prejudice.

It is like checking calves, measuring them. As if while they have been away from our care, we have feared for their progress, their feeding and their watering. My hands are trembling as they rest lightly on the slight shoulders of the boy. There is a shivering in my stomach, I am almost sick for a moment. Perhaps it is the stooping over, he is so small and neat. His face is as clear of blemishes as the surface of a well. Such a smile, an excellent smile like a person might draw, and indeed I am sure his grandfather Matt, as a respite from teaching those ungrateful children in Ringsend, has often drawn him, he is so suited to sitting still. As good as a landscape.

It is true that I don't really understand what a girl is, though I was one myself in the long ago. To look at me I am sure there is no trace of that, no lingering section of me which would tell you that once I ran about the lanes of Kelsha, Kiltegan and Feddin as slight as a twist of straw.

'Am I very much bigger?' says the boy almost sadly, as if catching my thoughts.

'You are not,' I say, laughing my laugh. 'You are most certainly not. But you have sprung up a little.'

'How I will ever get to the top of my father's head I do not know,' he says.

'Is that your ambition?'

'Daddy says one day I will be as tall as him. But he doesn't want me taller. He says I will have to leave home if I grow taller.'

'Perhaps you will not grow taller.'

'Oh, I am sure I will,' he says sadly, all three foot of him.

'I think your sister might get there before you,' I say, and the girl smiles in sudden triumph.

'He would not like that,' she says.

'Who?'

'Him,' she says, meaning, I suppose, her brother.

The boy gazes at the might of his sister. There is a look in his eyes of simple fear. I do not understand the fear at all.

'You will need to eat your cabbage,' I suggest to him.

'Now?' he says doubtfully.

'No, now you will go to bed. The owl is awake in the wood. Time for mortals to be a-bed.'

The whole of the world is still. The beech trees along the border of the wall are quiet tonight. The woods themselves must be halted above on the ridge. And there is no thrashing about of branches to disturb the children, who, after all, are city children, and need time to adjust, and not just to the butter. Salted, unsalted, that is the difference, salted and unsalted life. They cannot be immediately at home, it is not possible, no matter how deeply I revere them.

I thank God for the windless night.

The children are in their bedroom sleeping as deep as river stones. I am thinking of the little boy in his nest of sheets and blankets. The sheets are like white card they are so starched.

I was so eager to make their bedclothes agreeable and nice, I am afraid I was a bit loose-handed with the starch bottle. No matter. The old brown water bottle softens them a little. I know he will have his small feet set on it, in a kind of friendly fashion.

He has an odd attitude to mere objects,

he imparts characteristics to them. The water bottle hence is his friend. The old blue coverlet, with the scenes of country life stitched onto it, is his friend. He has greeted everything in the house with a kind of satiated longing. I wonder what his dreams might be.

Perhaps he sees the long road to Kelsha unwinding in his sleep, the sparkling hedges, the unknown farms. A little boy's thoughts, what may they be?

The kettle is back off the flames on its grubby crane — the grease of cooking defeats even us — because I could not be tempted to tea now so late, as it might have me stiff in the bed with sleeplessness, which would be an awful occasion. I will be depending now on sleep for my recuperation, the friendly sister of sleep.

A day of hardship is a long day, good times shorten the day, and yet a life in itself is but the breadth of a farthing. I am thinking these thoughts, country thoughts I suppose, old sayings of my father.

My father liked just as much as myself the empty spectacle of the fireplace, or did until the great restlessness took a hold of him. After that nothing suited him.

Everything seems far away as I sit there in the gloom of the lowering turf. Everything seems to stand off in the distance, like those deer that slip from the woods at dusk to crop the soft grasses. I am thinking about nothing, slipping from one idle thing to the next as one does beside a fire. For instance it strikes me for no reason at all that the deer are in their Sunday coats, every day of the year.

Jack Furlong the rabbit man goes in after the rabbits but I know he would not hunt the deer. There are thousands of rabbits up on the knolls where the trees end. He is a tender man but it is his work to kill them.

Billy Kerr would harass the deer if there was any profit to himself in doing so, as he is a man without qualities. There is probably a Billy Kerr, or someone like him, in all human affairs. Otherwise all would be well, continually.

But no life is proof against the general tears of things. And as I sit there alone between the sleeping children and the sleeping Sarah, the coverlet over her face in our bedroom behind me, I am not thinking of Billy Kerr in any especial way. My mind is drifting, there is a measure of ease. The children sleep without a sound, the ashes of the turf collapse with a familiar noise the size of mice. I can hear over my head in the wooden loft the tiny dance steps of the real mice as they cross and re-cross in a strange regularity, always going to the limits of the loft and heading back across the boards intently, as if drawing a great star on the dusty boards.

After a while I am disturbed by a little mewling sound, which at first I imagine is coming in from the henhouse. It is built up against the south gable of the house or nearly, and we are therefore neighbours to the hens.

But I fancy it is not the hens. Hens make a sound of outrage when the foxes come down from the trees. This is not a sound of henny outrage, but something softer and darker. I start up from my chair when I realise it is coming from the children's room.

To their door I dart, lifting the metal latch as gently as old practice can manage, and peer into the glistening dark. What little light follows me in the door now finds the turns and angles of things, the dull brass on the beds and the like. I wonder is it the boy awake and confused by the strange surroundings? But no, it is not he, but the soft swan of the girl in her white nightdress. Her covers are down in the chill bath of stray lights, her little legs are up at the knees, her head of dark hair twists and turns, and out of her red mouth issues the curious sound of something akin to distress.

Of course I creep over to her. I know it is wrong to wake a sleepwalker, but she is not walking. All the same she looks like she is awake in another setting, dreaming she is somewhere with her eyes open. The eyes are not looking at me or anywhere, they are focused on invisible things.

Perhaps I ought to wake Sarah because Sarah for all her silence often knows the solutions to matters that to me seem tangled and dark. The limbs of the little girl are rather beautiful in the murky light, she reminds me of something, maybe my own girlhood, maybe my own early softness and slightness, before my tussle with polio. I do not know.

The little girl cries out. I risk putting a hand on her forehead and immediately her eyes change as I stoop there over her. She lets out a pure thin scream, I never heard the like.

'What is it, what is it?' I say.

'The tiger is in the room,' she says.

'There are no tigers in Wicklow,' I say, but, God help me, I gaze about nevertheless in the fear of seeing one. 'Bless us, child, there is nothing. Now,' I say, sitting on the edge of the little bed and stroking her head. Her hair is soft as first grasses. 'Now, there is nothing to fear. Here you are in Kelsha. You are safe and sound tucked up in your bed. I am here and Sarah.'

The little girl starts to cry. It is a slight, distant, private crying, melancholy and affecting. I am ashamed of myself suddenly for thinking littler of her earlier than her brother. My heart goes out to her, as whose could not?

'Oh, Auntie Anne,' she says.

'Oh, dear,' I say.

I gather her in my arms. She is only gentle bones. To think a person is a soul wrapped in this cage of bones. What an arrangement, how can we possibly be protected?

'I am very afraid of the tiger,' she says. 'I am glad he is not here.'

'That's the truth,' I say.

She looks at me. She pushes me away a little, as if to see me better. Her own eyes are more accustomed to the dark of that room. There is a world of words in her look, I can almost see her brain struggling. But it is too much for her. Perhaps she does not have words for what she wants to say. Instead she says something else, something simple, that all the children of the world have said in their time, to their mothers and the like. But I had never had it said to me.

'I love you, Auntie Anne,' she says.

The wolf of pride smiles in my breast.

'Oh, I'm sure,' I say, as pleased as I have ever been, and tuck her back down into the bed. And I laugh.

And she laughs.

'You go off to sleep now,' I say. 'I'll sit here till you do. God knows.'

And, just as I had mentioned to the boy, the barn owl, that roosts not in the barns, but in the tallest pine at the margin of the woods, calls out one haunting, memory-afflicted note.

Chapter Two

Daylight opens the farm wide, the fearful shadows flee from the damp trees, the pony wakes in his standing, the calves clamber up in the calf byre. I stand in the yard at the rain barrel, holding the enamel jug, stilled by the unexpected veil of sunlight thrown over everything. There is almost heat in it, that May sunlight. Even the cobbles lose their toes of shadows, and the water at the top of the barrel lies in a loose mirror.

I can feel the heat getting into the very fibres of my blouse, a slight heat addressing a woman of slight heat. My bones are grateful where they lie in their weary slings. I lift my face to the light and am amazed again at what great pleasures there are to be had on this earth.

I have lain beside a sleeping Sarah all night, sleeping myself the odd time, trying not to turn or moan and wake her, and was despondent in my thoughts, despite the coming of the children. I became fearful again for their safety, for our ability to guard them, and almost cursed their father for leaving them. Such were the thoughts

26

of the night, banished by this stripling sun.

I plunge the jug down through the film of browned leaves that have come from the gutter despite that Billy Kerr was supposed to clean it, and the rainwater floods in. With the proper gesture the jug can now be lifted without any debris in it, a small triumph of the morning. Out comes Sarah from the kitchen, closing the half-door behind her, with the big basin of grain. She grabs a fistful of it and calls out to the hens, though they are fast still in their coop. Perhaps she does it to excite them.

'Chuck-chuck, chuck-chuck, chuck-chuck.'

'Sarah, dear, you haven't washed.'

'I'll wash in a minute, Annie.'

'You have your blouse on now over your wrists and you haven't washed them.'

'No more than yourself.'

'But I have the sleeves rolled to the elbows in readiness.'

'The hens are hungry.'

She pulls the wooden hasp on the henhouse and hauls open the old door. It is another thing that needs fixing, for it touches the ground and the rain is eating it from underneath. Billy Kerr again. But then Billy Kerr is not our man, but the man of the Dunnes of Feddin, my three cousins below. We would have our own man but that we can't afford a whole man all the time. I would not pay a regular wage anyway to Billy Kerr, because his work is dubious.

The cock rushes from the coop in all his confused annoyance and begins to march up and down the yard, nearly running he is. The poor fellow looks like a girl in a rusty tutu all the same, a ballerina. And now his ladies follow him out slowly, bruised-looking from the darkness of the coop, less sure, less eager. They love Sarah, you would think by the way they see her now and crowd against her, and she shakes her wrist of grain at them, the wrist she has not washed, and when it hits the stones like hailstones and leaps about, the hens fasten their beaks into it, a-worrying the whole time, you would think by their glassy eyes, that they will not get enough to fill their bellies.

'Get back, get back, get back!' cries Sarah, which is her cry to them these days, because her eyes are failing and she fears to tread on them.

'Why do you do that?' I said to her, just a few weeks previous.

'Because I cannot see them,' she said.

'You must go up to Dublin to see the eye doctor,' I said.

'I couldn't see him, either,' she said, laughing.

'We must make arrangements,' I said. 'It is only sensible.'

'I must manage for the minute,' she said. 'A doctor is a pricey item.'

And since then she does seem to be managing well enough. She is devising strategies, other ways of seeing perhaps. I do not always understand her. At night she pulls the blanket over her face and sleeps under it. In the watches of the night when I have foolishly drunk tea late, and lie awake, I hear her muttering and squawking under the blanket. Now and then she thrashes around, as if she were a marching soldier.

She seems to see well enough when she is asleep, whatever about her waking difficulties.

She marches slowly at the hungry hens, throwing the dampened grain. When she throws it against the sunlight, its colour lightens. Her big hand flashes with grain. Her legs are like the slender pillars of the courthouse in Baltinglass, advancing.

'When you are finished there,' I say, 'come in and wash your wrists like a good woman.'

In I go to the kitchen, closing the half-door behind me, in case the hens might follow me in, and through the kitchen to our bedroom. Into our basin in the bedroom I pour the residue of the rain.

Such water you could not drink. But to plunge in my two hands and lift it, and bang it against my cheeks — my underskin sparkles, it feels like. I see things for an instant — things of summer, rooks racketing out of the trees, heavy heated leaves flashing. Then the room again, the simple wooden room, our only carpeting the chill of May that lies across the floor and seems to seep up through my stout shoes.

Those sleepy heads within, I must wake them. Into their bedroom I go softly to steal a look at their sleeping.

The little girl is peaceful now. She lies on the bed as if gliding across some unseen surface, as if skating, one leg leading the other, the toes pointing.

The boy has neither turned nor stirred you would think, but is ramrod in the starched sheets. Everything is undisturbed, his small head lies in the pillow like an egg in soft earth. I will hardly need to make his bed tonight, except that you must turn down the sheets to retrieve the clay water bottle. I am half laughing at the sight.

'Come on up,' I whisper, stirring at their

forms with my fingers, not tickling but waking them. 'It is time to rise. The hens are fed. Come on up,' I say, 'it is nearly half past six already.'

The little girl opens her eyes suddenly and looks at me. Perhaps she was already awake, and kept her eyes closed to tease me.

'Half six,' she says, 'Auntie Anne, no human being ever rose at half six.'

'Well, you are forgetting your country manners,' I say. 'If our work is not done by ten, the day is wasted.'

'Do we have a lot of work then?'

'Only to watch me and Sarah, and mind Shep doesn't eat your toast.'

'I'll get up at half six for toast,' she says.

'So will I,' says the boy, with his brown farthings for eyes watching me.

'Did you have good dreams?' I ask him.

'I did,' he says. 'Perfect dreams.'

'And what did you dream in the night?'

'I dreamed our daddy carried us on his back, the both of us, and we were laughing like monkeys.'

'Where did you ever see monkeys laughing?'

'In the zoo,' he says, severely, poised at the end of the bed, shivering a little.

They sit in to the makeshift table by the

31

fire, and I hold out their bread on a long iron fork, and soon the turf flames begin to paint the slice with a soft brown.

'Now,' says the girl, 'do you hear that?'

'What?' says the boy.

'I told you the cricket would still be there in the stones.'

And they cock their ears dutifully to the cricket and sure enough the cricket sings for them.

'You'd think he'd like to be out in the fields singing, not singing in here with us,' says the boy.

'You would think,' I say. 'But there is no telling with crickets.'

'Do I like the sound at all? I don't know,' says the boy. 'Is a cricket like a snake or what is it like?'

'It's just a little thing with folded wings.'

'Like an angel,' says the boy.

'Well, aye, I suppose, like an angel in the wall.'

Then the rattling of the latch and Billy Kerr puts his head in the door. It is very early for him and anyway we have sent down no message to him to come up.

'Ah, there you are, Annie,' he says. 'Where's Sarah at this hour?'

There you are, Annie, where's Sarah? I

32

don't know what it is, but I look at him with accustomed suspicion. He is forty-five and his appearance is his own business. But I don't like the head of him, the scraggy red hair and the black stubble on his chin. I don't like his small stature and the set of clothes on him that might give pause to a tinker before he put them on. Of course they are work clothes and I shouldn't be so harsh. But it is the air of the man, the confidence grounded on so little evidence for confidence. Even though he has swept off his cap it is the same as if he hasn't bothered. Anyway he waves his cap at me like he was airing it, like he was drying it of sweat in the warm kitchen after the long walk uphill along the green road from Feddin.

'If you don't see her in the yard, I don't know where she is. Don't you go creeping about. It is early morning and she hasn't even washed herself.'

'I don't see her,' he says, looking back out into the yard. 'No, I don't.' For a full half minute he stands there, showing us the heathery hair on the back of his head.

Silence has fallen on the children the way it does when they don't know a person, and they are staring quietly at him like two blades of shovels. At last he swivels his head again and seems to see the children for the first time.

'Whose are these girls?' he says.

'They're not both girls. It's my nephew's children.'

'Ah, yes. The boy is not hardy yet! Is he four?'

The little boy looks up curiously.

'He is nearly five,' I say, like a lawyer to the defence.

'Down for a few days?' he says airily.

I am not inclined to give him information, harmless though the information is. And anyway everyone will know hereabouts soon enough. But information is a gift of sorts, and I feel ever niggardly towards him. So I say nothing with an easy air, not to give offence and yet not to give satisfaction.

'Ah, anyway,' he says. 'Pleased to meet ye.'

Then he hovers there. There is no end to his ability to hover. I have seen him hovering over a shovel when he ought to have been sluicing out a ditch, with yards of a flooded field behind him.

It suddenly strikes me that his eye is on the black kettle that rattles with heat over the turf. I concentrate my efforts on not glancing in the same direction, or I can be accused of rudeness later, down in the village where no doubt he laughs about my temperament.

Everyone knows my grandfather was once the steward there, and a tall, lofty-minded person he was, that the likes of Billy Kerr would not have dared address directly, and if he had, would have been given no answer. But those days are gone and blasted for ever, like the old oak forests of Ireland felled by greedy merchants long ago.

There are some who remember such things in their own way. They like to see me hanging on the mercy of Sarah, if that is what I am doing. They like to see a woman with nothing between herself and the county home but the kindness of a cousin, a woman whose relatives were kings of Kelsha one time. *Poor Annie Dunne*, they must say, if they are kind. They will find other things to say, if they are not. Well, if we were something then, I am nothing now, as if to balance such magnificence with a handful of ashes. Our glory alas was before any of those mad gunmen, De Valera and his crew, thought to throw everything over with a dark frenzy of blood and murder. Before all the wars, all the upheavals, the uprisings and the civil disturbances, thirty long years ago, the very things that destroyed my own father's mind. For my father was a simple policeman in seditious times, and it did for him conclusively.

Oh, Billy Kerr knows all this, if he knows nothing else, as he hovers there expertly amid the gleaming colours admitted by the door.

'What's up with you, Billy Kerr?' says Sarah, coming in the door behind him, so he has to dislodge himself off the threshold. To my surprise his manner changes. He is very mollifying and stooping with her.

'How d'you do, Sarah?' he says.

'I do the same as most people at first light, bestir myself and set about my business.'

'Of course you do.'

'Your washing water is in the bedroom, Sarah,' I say.

'Thank you, Annie,' she says, with especial kindness. 'Shut the lower door, Billy Kerr, or you'll have the hens in.'

Stooping, stooping. I am disturbed. I was ever disturbed I suppose by a man coming to the house. Perhaps it is characteristic, or historical. Half the castle regiment used to call at my father's door for my little sister Dolly, and by heavens I never tired of seeing them on their way. I would not see her go with a soldier. And as for the young policemen that desired the same happy thing, they got even shorter shrift, because well I knew the extent of their wages, by listening to my father for twenty odd years. I would barely open the door to them. And Dolly used to accuse me of jealousy, but if it was that, it made no essential difference. She had to be protected. And Maud getting into a big moil of anxiety about it, as if worrying alone would fix such a thing.

'What is it you came up to us to do?' I ask him, as his eyes follow Sarah disappearing into our bedroom, rolling up the grainy sleeves of her blouse. We will be rubbing at those sleeves now on washday and she will regret her indifference then.

'Hah?' he says, as if that were English enough for me.

'Is there a job you're midway through, or what? I don't remember sending down for you, if I may say so without offence.'

'Sending down for me?' he repeats, smiling, not bothering further to express his mockery.

'Well, we have a world of work,' I say.

'I have my own work below,' he says. 'But I was of a mind to come and visit you.'

'Visit? Is it visiting this is? At seven o'clock in the morning on a mere weekday? With the calves to muck out and the pony and the cows to milk and the water to fetch?'

'Winnie Dunne below thought it might be all right. That you might have something wanting to do. A fence or a heavy weight for moving. Or the like.'

'Is it shillings you're after? Because there isn't a halfpenny in the house till I sell my eggs in Kiltegan.'

'I don't depend on your shillings, Annie Dunne,' he says, and laughs.

I am a little flustered now, confused. It's an ill thing to mention money before a labouring man. I don't know why I was betrayed into such a foolish remark. I am angry with myself. But I don't know what the man wants. His bravery in front of me is confounding.

Now Sarah comes out again all spick and span from her washing. She has pinned her nice white hair into a bun. Usually it washes about her cheeks like hanging ivy. She has used the old brown hair hook that my mother left behind her. My mother pinned her exhausted hair with it in her last illness. I found it on her bedside table at close of day, and so kept it in her memory.

Sarah heads for the boiling kettle and relieves it of its turmoil by pushing it back on the crane, and she scours out the teapot with a splash of that water and then drops in four spoons of tea and wets it as suddenly as she can with a deluge of water. The four spoons don't inspire. A spoonful for each drinker and one for the pot. The children are not interested in tea. So in the normal manner of things she would put in only three spoonfuls.

Billy Kerr is emboldened by all this to step further in from the door and he is smiling widely at Sarah, who probably is paying him no heed. He can count as well as me, we all went to the same school in our day, though he went ten good years, and more, it must be, after either of us. He is nodding his head as if someone has said something that he is assenting to. But no one has spoken. Sarah puts three blue and white cups on the table and sets the pot by them and the bowl of sugar lumps and the jug of milk. The broken light feasts on the turns of the glaze on these poor objects. Sarah lifts her face and without either happiness or sadness, or seemingly anything in between, says,

'Tea for thirst.'

'Aye,' says Billy Kerr, and comes in further again.

I go over and take the arm of the little boy and shepherd him from the table. I cannot drink tea in this little muddiness of confusion.

'I'll fill the bucket,' I say, as neutral as an ambassador.

'Oh, will you not drink your tea?' says Sarah, genuinely surprised.

'Put the cosy on it, Sarah, dear.'

'All right, Annie,' she says.

I find myself nodding to Billy Kerr. It is difficult to leave a room without even a bare nod, but I would rather I had omitted it.

'All right,' he says, whatever he means by it. It is just an echo of Sarah maybe. 'Good day to you, my little bucko,' he says to the boy as the child passes, being towed by myself, my defeat no doubt plain and clear by the redness I feel flaring on my cheeks.

And I go out into the yard, trailing doubt like a comet trails a fiery tail.

Chapter Three

I stand in the yard as still as a cow with her calf when the air presses down heavy in the summer. The bucket creaks ever so slightly in my hand.

What is this growing old, when even the engine that holds our despair and hope in balance begins to fail us?

She is old, yes, Sarah Cullen, as I am myself. She was born in the last flutter of the old century, in the winter of 1898. I was born two years later, it is the same gap oddly enough that is between the children.

She was a beautiful little girl, with a tousle of wheaten hair. Nothing afflicted her, joy jumped in her marrow.

There is only a whisper of time between then and now, it seems to me. The clock of the heart does not follow the one on the mantelpiece.

Oh, I thank God for Sarah Cullen. I have spent these years with her now, after Matthew turned me from the house in Dublin. It was a crime I will ever hold against him. To take up with another woman when my sister Maud was only two years in her grave. I did briefly have a hope that he might be glad of a female to serve his household, now poor Maud was gone. But that was not to be. He wished, it seems, to marry again, and he was not interested in his sister-in-law with her bowed back. While Maud lived, he used to jest, 'Annie, you carry the moon on your back,' which was a nice thing to say. But I do not think it looked to him like the moon when his mind turned to marrying a second time. But there. It is an ill story, maybe even a filthy story. That was a terrible time, and Sarah Cullen took me in.

All the anxiety of these recent years has been the fear of losing my last niche in the world, the left side of Sarah's bed, and this little farm. All I have brought to her is a few of the hens, those Rhode Island Reds kicking about the yard, an almost laughable thing, and the strength of my own body. My fortune currently is the mere strength left to me, and the knowledge I have of the tasks of each day, of the byre, of the dairy, of the dunghill, of the well, of the fire. If that went, all my value would be at naught.

The county home is a fearful place. That is where the homeless and the country destitute go, the withered girls and the old bachelors finally maddened by the rain. This I know, because I have seen it with my own eyes. It is a terrible fact to me that my poor father died there, alone and astray in his head.

The Wicklow rain has madness in it like an illness, an ague.

I am thinking these thoughts as I stand, stymied, in the yard with the boy. The bucket is in my hand but I cannot go forward.

I can see, beyond the boundary of the green road, the stooped figure of Mary Callan, returning from the well.

She is a devil for disturbing the mud and the twigs at the bottom of any well. It is a penance to have to share a well with her, as we do. In the old days it was said that the first draw of water in the morning pulled the luck of the well into your bucket. She is certainly old enough to believe that, for she must be in her nineties. She has a field and a milking cow and a house with one room, and now the luck of this day in her brimming bucket. It will be an hour at least before the muck settles.

Sometimes too she brings that old blackened kettle of hers straight to the well and fills it. It leaves such a scum on the surface. You cannot truly clean a vessel that touches upon the fire, and I am sure she makes no attempt to clean it. She is a bad, old-fashioned woman.

But that is not the only thing that keeps me there. I feel like a woman that has left her gloves on the bus, beautiful soft leather gloves on the Dublin bus, and does not know it immediately, but *senses* powerfully her loss. It is that I have left Sarah alone with Billy Kerr.

The boy is looking up at me in puzzlement.

'We must go back in, child.'

And back in I go, the boy still anchored by my hand, from the pleasing sunlight to the kitchen draped in its share of shadows. The little girl has already wandered off.

Sarah stands with her back to the turf warming her long bones and Billy Kerr sits in an easy and accustomed manner on one of the stone benches in the elbows of the fireplace. Neither is speaking. There is a sort of tea-drinking silence that country people have perfected over centuries. A lot can get said in those silences, they are dangerous elements.

'What is it, Annie?' says Sarah.

'I can't get the water now, Mary Callan has beaten me to it. That's the danger of delay,' I say, nodding to Sarah. 'Now, that cow of hers,' I say, but Billy Kerr interrupts me with a look of surprise.

'What's the matter with her cow?' says Sarah.

'What, Annie Dunne?' says Billy Kerr, sceptically.

'Blood in the milk,' I say, authoritatively. 'It should by rights be slaughtered.'

'You think so, Annie Dunne?' he says. 'That's a mite unchristian. She owns nothing else. She lives from that cow.'

'She's a dirty old woman that lives in filth, is the truth,' I say, and immediately regret the flush of anger in my throat. My father used to say, some people misinterpret friendliness for foolishness. No danger of that in my case, I expect. But there is another foolishness, the foolishness of the angry woman.

'You wonder why do I speak for her?' says Billy Kerr. 'Indeed, and I hardly know her, though she has lived there across your green road for all the years of my life. I am not acquainted intimately with her cow neither, having seen it only in the distance. But, the fact is, she is my mother's cousin, and a clean-living sensible woman. Nanny Callan, she is called by our lot.'

'Blood in the milk,' I say again, without any relish, the gate of talk pushed open for myself, sadly. 'I am afraid of what she leaves in the well. She has only the one bucket, I know, for milking and fetching water.'

'I'm sure Mary Callan has more than the one bucket,' says Billy Kerr. 'Don't the tinkers go about with buckets for twopence? Anyway, she is my cousin. That should be enough for you, to quieten your talk of her.'

'Sure everyone is cousins here,' I say, exasperated, more by myself than by him. What do I care for his damn cousinage. Nothing.

'He might be a cousin of yourself, Annie,' says Sarah, in a reasonable, innocent tone, not by any means feigned.

'Well, I hope then, not too close, for the purposes he has in mind!'

'What do you mean, Annie?' she says, with her guileless open face, with a curtain of fright down it now.

'He knows what I mean.'

'I do not,' he says, with an air that would convince a judge.

'Oh, he does,' I say.

But I am not at all sure. And Sarah won't look at me now. It is not her fault. She has fallen a-dreaming. It is her trick, her way of — I do not know exactly, of putting up with me, maybe. God help me! It is like Billy Kerr to rattle a person's head. I must get him from the house. Oh, he delights in vexing me.

'Mary Callan wouldn't have much truck with two-pences and tinker's buckets,' I say, like a leaking tap. There is polite scorn in my voice that would sap the strength of a lion. 'There was never any money in her house, I'd be sure and certain. She is that old sort of cottier. The walls of that little one-roomed house are only mud. The hungers of the last century took her lot. In 1872, it is well remembered, when there was half a famine here, it nipped and tucked her kin, seven or eight of them that lived there. She and her father was left. She but a waif that time of fifteen years. She is said to be one hundred and two years old.'

What am I talking about? It is like the geese gabbling.

'Annie Dunne,' says Billy Kerr. 'You are a humorous woman, in a manner of speaking.'

'We will go down to Kiltegan in a while,' I say to Sarah. 'Don't linger there too long.'

' "The hungers of the last century",' says Billy Kerr, 'that's very amusing! That's a turn of phrase now you don't hear often.'

'I must go out and harness the pony,' I say, nearly weeping from my own — stupidity.

'I'll harness the pony for you, and bring the trap up to him,' says Billy Kerr, suddenly and inconveniently polite.

'Please do not,' I say.

'Well, as you like. If you are going, I could use the drive down,' he says, with the same fake pleasantry. 'There's a parcel at the public house that came down on the Dublin bus for one of my women.'

My women. He is the mere slave of the Dunnes of Feddin. If Lizzie Dunne heard him say that. *My women.* Of course you could interpret his words a number of ways, that is his safety. Oh, I am not up to his cleverness. *Well, as you like.* He incenses me. I will not have him lording it in our old trap, at any cost.

'You will have to walk down the way you came,' I say, as neutral as I can, 'because it will be a good while before we are ready.'

'But you're only after saying —' he begins, for the first time unsteadied, but I am too quick for him.

'Where is the little girl?' I say, changing the topic roughly, but it will serve my purpose.

'She is inside in the room,' says Billy Kerr, though it wasn't him I asked.

'Well, then,' I say, and march in there, boy and all. Billy Kerr says something in my wake to Sarah but I don't catch it.

The little girl stands on the bed, with her back to me. She wears her flower-print summer dress and a knitted green cardigan that is beginning to be too small for her.

The sunlight in the small window beams down on her like a yard lamp. She is a small creature growing by inches. She does not know the world. She does not know her road ahead.

In the first second of putting my face into the room I imagine she has a burden on her back. Not like my own remnant of polio, but a heavy shadow. Then she moves and the picture is gone, a trick of the sunlight and my own mind.

Her head turns to look at me, and her eyes show their tiny stars. I am arrested there by her. And even the boy, with all the helpless twitching-about of a four-year-old, albeit nearly five, imitates my stillness. Suddenly, in a manner just as enlivening as sunlight, she smiles. A clear, unbroken, innocent smile.

'What are you doing in here, smiling like

49

the Cheshire cat and standing on beds?'

'I am glad to see you, Auntie Anne,' she says. 'I was lonely.'

'Well, I wasn't gone so far,' I say. 'We only ventured out to the well. And even at that we were baulked. Next time, just think of following me.'

'I am glad we are here in Kelsha,' she says. 'I am just glad.'

'I am glad you are glad,' I say. 'Come and help me put the harness on that wild fella Billy.'

'On that interesting fellow out there with Sarah?' says the boy.

'No. It would be impossible to get a harness on that fella. No, on Billy the pony. We will be half an hour readying him up, by which time I hope and trust Billy Kerr will be gone.'

But he is leaving even as I come back out into the kitchen. His mysterious visit completed, he sets off with a swagger down the yard and out onto the road. Paused at the half-door, I watch him go, pitching along indifferently. He has hips like sharp buckets.

When I glance back, Sarah's long passive face in the kitchen tells me nothing. She puts the used crockery aside for later washing and sets to to scrub the kitchen table. Since Billy Kerr barely set an elbow on it, I am surprised by her extremity of attention. Her long arms cover the pale, soft surface, the brush making a noise of tumbling straw, up and down, across and back. Now and then she dips the brush in salted water, and away again, her bared arms bleakly flashing.

It is eloquent enough, but of what I do not know. I resolve to question her later in bed, before the cover goes up over her face, and she is at her ease. I have a great respect for her silence. I do not like to badger her. Whenever by chance I do, the door of her face bangs in the wind, you might say, and she will talk nonsense then, frightened nonsense.

'I think I will bring the children with me down to Kiltegan and fetch our packet of tea.'

'You might have put up with the help of Billy Kerr so,' she says, conversationally.

'Ah, well,' I say. 'It will interest the children to assist me. Let him walk back the way he came.'

'It is all the same to me whether he walks or drives,' she says. 'I was thinking of your back.'

'My back is fine,' I say, blushing to the roots of my hair.

'It is of course,' she says.

'Will I get sugar also?'

'Don't,' she says. 'We have done well enough with that.'

'Sugar and tea. Don't we live like lords, Sarah, indeed and we do.'

Sarah laughs. Her laugh is thick and chesty, like blackberries beginning to bubble in the big pot, when we are making preserves in the autumn. As for myself, it was the opinion of old Thomas Byrne, that swept the castle yard long ago, that I have a laugh like a sheepdog's bark.

She stands in the kitchen, straight as a bittern, wielding the scrubbing brush. She is laughing again.

'You know, Annie, the only people that live like lords are lords,' she says.

She sets the scrubbing brush down on the table and puts her hands on her upper knees and is laughing. Her whole form is bent over as she does so, in a perfect show of lightness and gaiety. The children are shocked into delight and begin to laugh also, looking up at me. And I do not fail the moment, I laugh heartily, highly, laughing, laughing, yes, yes, as Thomas Byrne said, like a blessed sheepdog, 'Wher, wher, wher.'

The truth is, there is not much between

the characters of Billy Kerr and Billy the pony, only I don't have to hitch the former to the trap, which is a job of some difficulty.

Myself and the little ones pass the muddled mess of Shep, asleep in a suntrap on the yard. He barely stirs his addled snout. He is more slothful than a sloth and we have no sheep for him anyway.

We reach the dark rectangle of the byre entrance and the children peer in at Billy with admiration. They do not understand his true nature, but that is the mercy of children. He looks back at them from the glooms of the byre, his blunt front-face smeared with a sort of dampened anger.

He is a strong Welsh cob of small stature that Sarah bought at the fair in Baltinglass, and she reveres him because it was actual money she gave for him, pound notes that her mother left her. He is a grey, a pure grey, to give him his due, without a hint or a speckle of anything else. But of late I have begun to fear his strength. He brims with a kind of inconvenient hatred.

It is in his eyes, the black stone of them. His life with us, it seems, whatever his ambitions were, does not suit him. Perhaps we do not take him out often enough. Perhaps it is the countryside offends him.

Gingerly I heave the heavy gear onto his back, conscious I admit of the help I have foregone from Billy Kerr, in my arrogance.

'There is a slime all over the leather,' says the girl.

'No,' I say, panting, my back hurting. 'It is a preserving grease is on it, against the rain.'

'It is dirty,' she says, 'and it is on my cardigan.'

'Do you not want to drive in the trap?' I say, rebuking her only because I am in pain.

'Oh, I do,' she says. 'I do.'

It is lovely all the same how the harness sits on Billy. It is well moulded to him, over the years. I relish the fatness of his girth, like a well-fed man. He smells of dry straw and moist dung and his own strange smell, of his hair and of his hide. There is something of the lion about him. He has more style than Shep, anyhow. But that he looks like he wants to kill you, you could admire him.

Out onto the green road then, the two excited children facing each other on the benches behind me, the fields and woods about us rising and falling slightly. And Billy's hooves throwing up little plates of mud. It is the sound I make between teeth and tongue that makes him really go. We stream down the green river of grass, the children gripping the seats under them.

I give a brief wave to Mrs Kitty Doyle in her yard. She is bringing an apronful of rough food to her pigs. I can hear them squealing like doors in their stone pen. In one of her barns lurks an abandoned trap, I can just make it out as we rattle by, its high shape left in with the bales of straw. It moulders there, the shine slipping slowly from the lamps. They are another lot that have purchased a motor car in these last years.

But the Hennigans' wheat is doing well, I notice, a beautiful crochet of fierce shoots thrown over an expanse of dark earth.

To the crossroads we come, where our mountain road gives way to the new tarmacadam. I have to put a damper on Billy's prancing. He has a nervous way about him here always, being heated up by the excitement of pouring down the hill.

I can see the distant back of Billy Kerr, traipsing the last few yards to the cow barns at the side of my cousins' house. Their farm lies in there behind the scraggling hedges. The house looks odd in its field of cow-created mud. The walls are brushed by damp and rain.

All the same, primroses and the green fountains of foxgloves crowd the mossy ditches. Gorse has just finished with its yellow fire along the hill behind. But Billy the pony does not wait for such miracles, on he lurches across the road, the wheels taking a new tune from the harder surface, our cheeks rattling from the shaking.

'Oh, come up, you wild mad pony, you,' I say, trying to put a break on him. I know in my heart he would like to canter now, to gallop, to carry all, himself and the unsatisfactory humans in the trap, away at a mad pace along the scattering pebbles, and throw the world into a gear of danger and terror. This I cannot let him do, so I am leaning back, standing in the trap, hauling him down into a flighty walk.

'Walk on, you tramp, you,' I say, deviously working the bit from side to side with the reins. But he is acting up worse than his usual wicked self, he is backing up on me now. The whole arrangement of trap and pony begins to bend in the middle, and I am suddenly afraid that we might be set into the ditch. The children behind me gasp with the irregular lurching and groaning of the shafts, striking about now like a huge tuning fork.

'Walk on, walk on,' I say, and I would curse at him but for the education of the children, the responsibility of that. And now Billy goes forth, and comes back in the next stride. He is intent on working some awful mischief on me. I could whip him now if I didn't dread the effect of the lash on him in this mood. I am crazy now in the head myself with worry and anger, banging about in the wooden seat.

'Stand, stand, you devil,' I say. 'Stand! Children, open the little gate and jump down from the metal steps. I do not think I can hold him.'

And the little girl in her greater wisdom takes charge of the boy and opens the little flap of plywood, and slides herself and the smaller one down, a considerable height for a child. But, thank the good Lord, in a trice both are standing bewildered on the grassy margin. The great engine, it must seem like to them, of the trap, with myself atop, buckles and bangs again.

'Children, stand there quietly,' I say. 'Oh, my heavens!'

Billy has worked the bit in between his teeth and clamped down hard and he has me now.

It is the catastrophe most to be feared. Sarah will never forgive me if I cannot retrieve him from his folly. For she values this foolish, perilous animal. I am abandoned now to horror, because I can almost see his next move. I can see it before maybe he even thinks it, being an animal of the instant, of the fleeting moment. Or maybe he has plotted this for years, eyeing me with those evil eyes. Here it is, the leap, the flurry, the coiling of his energy, the fire in his rotund belly flaring — and he is away, away, towards Kiltegan, with only foolish me to prevent him.

We run for a hundred yards and he gaily throws a shoe. The hardness of the road tears it from his hoof. It sails off over the hedges of Humewood, the old estate that was the centre of my forefathers' lives. He pays it no heed. Then, out of the tangled low trees to the left emerges like a Chinese rocket what at first I think is a wild boar, thrusting tusks and all. It is like a vision — one moment there is the peaceful untended hedgerow, and the next a hole blown through it, and this creature unfolding onto the road ahead.

But there are no wild boars in Ireland and anyway this creature calls and shouts and waves its arms. It lifts itself up and reveals its mysterious limbs and turns to my grateful amazement into Billy Kerr.

Now he stands in the centre of the Kiltegan road and raises his arms aloft and jumps and hoo-hoos at the fierce horse. By way of a characteristic answer, the pony violently halts and rears up with his front hooves showing, and comes down heavily again by force of the trap, and bucks his hind quarters once or twice, and rears again, caterwauling from his mouth, his tense jaws opened as wide as ever horse can. The trap is plunged to the left, and pitches so far over I am thrown from my precarious nest and fetched into the dock leaves and whatnot of the ditch.

'Get up if you can, Annie Dunne,' shouts Billy Kerr, 'and block his path behind. We'll have him then.'

So not knowing if I am dead or alive, I drag my old bones upright again and plant my feet on the ground and raise my arms. My whole body is trembling from fright and shock. My blue and white overdress is smeared with mud. My head bangs inside with blood, it feels like. Billy Kerr reaches up to grab at the flying mane of the pony, and grasps onto the halter, darkly growling, and suddenly is all soothing and soft.

'Now, now, easy up, easy up, there's the boy,' he says.

He caresses that pony like it was a little child humbled by catastrophe. Trembling himself, his very coat rippling and twitching, the pony calms at the honeyed words, stepping this way and that, like a drunk man. Billy Kerr rubs his broad neck.

'The children,' I say, and turn, and hobble back the road to where they dutifully have stayed.

Old Kelsha bones cannot lie down and count their bruises, certainly.

Chapter Four

We are lying, Sarah and me, like queens on a stone tomb. Night has fallen, and we are abed. The wind goes on with its counting of the leaves in the sycamores, a hundred and one, a hundred and two.

I can sense but not share the ease in her long bones. Going to bed, reaching the haven of our bed, is as releasing for her as death. Every day she dies, you might venture to say, into bed. Even I am grateful for the slack in the endless rope of labours. Soon enough it will pull tight on us again.

There she stretches, the clock of her heart tick-ticking, her blood with its thousand rivers under her mottled skin, her breasts rising and falling, lending the semblance of life to the country scene embroidered on the coverlet. It is a flock of deer depicted by her mother years ago, my mother's sister. They are running across hillocks of grass pursued by a black-coated hunter on a dark, thin horse. The landscape undulates like an enormous sea. Her breath whistles out between long teeth, thin lips.

Her big eyes are hooded, with a pattern of blue lines like tiny cups, and the coverlet hauled up as high as she can without bothering me.

We are Christian persons, imbued with the strange light of our Saviour, and to every one of us has been assigned by sleight of God an immortal soul. An immortal soul in all too mortal flesh. It is well for me to remember this, in this early watch of the night. I do not expect to sleep.

My head feels like the bed of a stream after the shock of floodwater. It is scoured out by the events of the day.

Billy Kerr. He has surprised me. He was deeply solicitous when the pony was calmed, and carried the little boy all the way back up the green road, while I led the girl by her slender paw. I was hobbling from the fall, but at the same time I was watching Billy Kerr, and how he laughed with the child and amused him, and plucked the foxgloves for him so he might burst them between his fingers. All memory of the terrible upset seemed to pass away under those subterfuges.

Then when we were all parked in the kitchen and the children on the settle by the helpful turf, Billy Kerr marched down to the crossroads and, not fearing at all, mounted the trap where he had the vehicle and its unrepentant animal tethered to a tree, and drove the contraption, with its one squeaking wheel, back up to us. The metal rim has been dislodged from the easeful balance of the spokes, the wraps of wood around the axle look askew. It will all be money to put right — money Sarah and myself do not have.

Billy Kerr stuck the trap in the hay barn, and Billy the pony in the byre, and both have a sort of disgraced look to them now, the wooden trap itself moping, with one of its lamps knocked into a lean from the force of the mishap.

I think of them both now, in the dark of the night, each alone, separated, the wife of the trap torn from the husband of the horse.

At length against the long impulse of the night I go out into the starry yard to comfort the long ropes of my muscles and the field sticks of my bones. I carry the bed heat on the surface of my skin and the soft breeze of the night shows great interest in me, raising the hairs on my arms. Before me lies the rough house of our sleeping pony, by my right arm the sleeping calves and the subdued wakefulness of the hens. It is foxes walk the sleep of hens, and keep them frittering with tiny noises. By my left, the slope of the old yard and the pillars of the gates. Beyond the black gape of the milking byre lurks the pleasing bulk of the two milking cows, Daisy and Myrtle, which Sarah did not have a chance to drive back out into the top field. If they do not eat the grasses they will not fatten their udders with the milk. Is it that Sarah grows forgetful, or was it the emergency that took that allotted box of time away from her?

It is past the midnight hour in this region of the south. We lie in here behind the mountains. It kept many things away and many things contained. Here in these districts built up great farms, with mostly English and Protestants to own them, and only the great force, the fist, of the old war here in Ireland sundered them.

Still the remnant power lies across our lives. For seven generations back, my family held the same job, right down the old century. It went from father to son without a break for a hundred years like a proper kingship. Everything that happened, and all that we were, stemmed from that sinecure, like a blossoming spray. Seven generations, seven men with seven lives to live, put themselves to be stewards of Humewood estate. They were kings of the labouring men. White Meg my grandfather is still talked of, a tall unseeing man, austere and rough, who would walk to the gates of Humewood, up the street of Kiltegan, and give neither hello nor comment to any passing person. I don't remember if I ever saw him, with my own child's eyes, but I seem to know, to feel, that he had a sense of his immense dignity, the fact that he had gained his place from his forebears, had filled their boots well, and would lie in his niche in the Catholic yard with a proper legacy of work and worth. He was called White Meg for his big white beard, an old-fashioned style that most men sported and that has passed away.

It is that not saying hello, that sense of being separate, that he has passed on to me, without much to justify it, except, we carried ourselves across the wide troubles of the land, and that my own father had the dignity of high office in the Dublin Metropolitan Police, and we were raised like favoured chickens in the great coop of Dublin Castle, where the Queens and Kings of England were pleased to quarter their policemen and their families, in those bright days, when the Viceroy would shake out his flags, and his coming and going was observed with due ceremony and banging of boots.

I stand out under the starlight. Surely the constellations are not satisfied with their names. Do they know they have been dubbed the Great and Little Bear, does Orion's Belt know it is Orion's Belt? My nightshift makes a little bleat in the wind, I rattle slightly like a sail. I love my land. It comes upon me like a second breeze, that strange and useless love. It is the place of Kelsha that o'erwhelms me, the arrangement of its woods, the offices of the yard, the animals in our care, the perfection and cleanliness of the very stones, all down to us.

The midden stands in its patch of dock leaves like an Egyptian pyramid. There is our quiet place behind the walls of the long outhouse where Sarah and myself make our toilet, wiping our rear ends with the grasses there perpetually damp. The habit in the cities of using newspapers is never as satisfactory, not by half, as those long, thin, green stems. And then cast into the pit, and the night soil from the potties carried there and likewise cast.

Under the starlight I stand, ruminating,

like a creature myself, an extra thing in the plenitude of the world. I know I am nothing. My pride is not based on my own engine, but is just a lean-to built on prejudice and leaning against anger. But this is not the point. God is the architect, and I am content there, sleepless and growing old, to be friend to his fashioned things, and a shadow among shadows. More rooted and lasting will be my crab-apple tree — some day, no doubt, another heart will give allegiance to it and its bitter fruit, gathering the tiny apples and crushing them in their season with the same passion and humour, laughing at the generosity of the tree, its ease and seeming happiness, its fertility, as I do. It is a mother of a thousand children, every year, like the offspring of the queen bee. The whole tree buzzes silently in the autumn with its excited fruit.

Now in the dark shales of the night it stands with its generous, bitter arms.

This is the happiness allowed to me.

If I am to rest at all it is time to try the bed again, for when the dark is broken by the fussy fingers of the dawn we must be up and about. *If your work is not done by ten, the day is wasted.* I go back into the house, closing the half-door behind me against the intrusion of the hens. Of course they are all fast in their coop, the closing of the door is a habit of the daylight. My favourite hen, who gives us sleek brown eggs aplenty, is with her fellow hens. In the hours of daylight I watch her, trim and pretty about the yard, plotting her secretive births. She likes to put her eggs in tricky places, and I have never seen her about that business yet. It needs an ingenious eye, a happy instinct to discover her rich warm haul. The boy believes he knows her secrets, which is both true and untrue — he is small enough for his eyes to creep under shelves of hay, struts of old wood. I call her Red Dandy, she is a Rhode Island Red, one of my own hens I am glad to say. Sarah has not such a layer. So I fasten the half-door, still letting the encouraging night breeze cross the upper portion and enter the dark kitchen. It is a sort of cleaning, that pleasant wind. And then I slip back beside the sleeping Sarah, between the stiff, starched sheets, under the bright coverlet with its perpetual scene. And I feel perfectly content, at peace with man and God. My slightly chilled skin feels the leak of parched heat that Sarah has made in the bed. Sleep tumbles in on top of me like a species of river swimming.

Is the dark troubled by our dreams? The whole district, the whole half of the world closed from the sun, dreaming. Men and women, sisters, brothers, in their allotted beds. The accidental nature of it all. My dreams are clear, like life really, whole and pure. I see my father there, the policeman, and my mother in her youth, when she loved to be with us, and counted herself the most blessed of women to have three girls and a little boy. We were her dry kingdom and her fallow field, where she let nothing grow, only the dallying sun was allowed there, to dance for us, to sing its dry song for us. So in my dreams I see her often, long, not beautiful, but calm and smiling. From this world of tears she was torn by a thinning disease, when my father was in his fiftieth year. It was a long, hard job for him to mind us. But in my dreams she is not dead, but precisely living, evenhanded and serenely just.

The summer offers a general peace, perhaps the very peace that passeth all understanding. God may have been thinking of the Irish winter when he wrote that in the good book. My spirit is altered by the deepening length of the days, the pleasant trick that summer plays, of suggesting eternity, when the light lies in the yard, and Shep is perpetually stricken by that light, the heavy weight of heat on those special days. Hopefully heaven itself will consist of this, the broadening cheer of light when I walk out into the morning yard. The stones already hot, softened by dawn. The rain deep in the earth seeps further down, and a lovely linen-like dryness afflicts the land. Grass becomes bright and separate, like a wild cloth. A crust appears on the dunghill. The piss of the calves dries in the gullies like spit on a heating griddle. Sleekness creeps over things, handles and insects. You can almost *hear* the work of the sun in those long, patient things, the buds of the crab-apple tree, the little hinges of the sycamores. How fresh and alive the leaves even, shouting with green, delighting in life. Stone and earth and wood, the make-up of our little hillside palace, where such as we abide.

How different our story would be if we were Greeks or Spaniards, and could count on that sunlight. But it is only a trick, for many a day of summer is sister to any winter day. And yet we embrace the trick, we live by it.

I have not fetched the lambs from their

lairs in the sheets, let them lie a little longer, they are still city children yet. Soon they will adjust to us, and rise with the cockcrow easily and full of go. The zinc bucket creaks in the hooks of my fingers, and I pass along the dew-drenched path to the well, sucking in the smells of clover and the queer fresh smell of the bread-and-butter bushes, a smell so slight you could miss it, a hair's breadth of a smell. The may sits heavily in the bushes this year. The slopes of Kelshabeg are all brightened by it, it is a free glory. My polka-dotted dress brushes the fringes of the taller grass, giving me a little line of wetness there, but I do not care. Though I am old I feel a skittering in my bones, a gratitude, an interest in this adventure, and I am speculating on the state of the well. Will she have been there before me, the wild witch across the road, and disturbed the mud, and washed some old working bucket there?

But all is clean and stately, the big sliced boulder of water lying in its crown of long grasses, the kneeling-stone dry and welcoming. So I dip my bucket there with secret expertise, not a grain of mud rises from the black bottom. The bucket drinks the water. Some boatmen, little black darting creatures, creep in on the deluge. Let them come, I do not care. They will keep the water stirred and good while it sits under its damp muslin cloth by the door.

For some reason I think of Mary Callan in her lone bed, no type of human body to lie at her side, in a filthy nest no doubt of fetid sheets. Perhaps on mere straw she lies, in the manner of the old days, when cottagers and the like could not stretch to such matters as linen. In the straw they all lay down, adults and children and many of them, and in the low part of the room the beasts lay down, the milking cow and a calf if they were lucky, and if more fortunate than most, the prized personage of the pig. It was the slope in the floor that kept the emissions of the animals well down from the sacred precinct of the hearth, where the human animals gathered and took their farthings of ease at nightfall. It is my suspicion that Mary Callan holds to these emergencies and customs yet. Should this awake a shadow of sympathy in me, such a dark, solitary life so near to our own? I suppose it should and does, but I damn her dirty bucket anyhow.

Now when the gloss of daylight has

brushed every stone, and the sun itself moved beyond the gable of the milking shed, and I have chastised Sarah for her neglecting to put Daisy and Myrtle back up to the grass, and given them an unaccustomed night under the spidery rafters, and I have roused the two children and brought porridge to their niche in the fireplace, where they lurk now with spoons like the mites they are, Billy Kerr comes in to us. I am not so surprised to see him, since he may have things to do to right the old trap, or some such plan, nor am I so vexed. The services of the previous day have given me a lingering endurance of him, with his round face speckled with unshaven hairs. His chin and cheeks are like wood infested with a damp bloom. There seems to be a big bone across his shoulders so he looks perpetually like a man with a wooden yoke for two buckets, except there are no buckets, only some mysterious invisible weight that stoops him slightly. As a woman with a hump myself, I would not care to see the children you would get off of such a man, no more than I would have cared to risk children out of myself, though the great need was there, certainly. It might well be crooked children he would give a woman.

No matter for that, Sarah greets him kindly and sets him at the scrubbed table and fetches tea to him again. Maybe he senses the relaxation in me, because he is not annoying or dark with me this day, but glances over at me and smiles in a brotherly fashion. Maybe he thinks the ring is in my nose now, the danger is less in me.

'That's a great mass of sunlight now,' he says, 'stretching the height of Keadeen mountain and I don't think we will see rain again for a week. So between the recent rain and the sun, anyone with potatoes sown will be happy. The Dunnes of Feddin have half an acre sown. They were sitting up with their boiled eggs this morning as happy as pigs in muck.'

'Why wouldn't they?' says Sarah. 'They're hard to work. Did you put in those spuds for them, Billy Kerr?'

'I did. The four worked side by side. We were fitting in spuds and singing. Good work.'

'Well,' says Sarah, edging the cup with its rings of blue and white closer to his hand because he has not drunk yet, 'it is a good thing to have the spuds to put in, and the ground, and the people to do the putting. Me and Annie will sow our own store soon, I am sure.'

'We most certainly will,' I say. 'Most certainly.'

The children sit in the niche of the fire, staring at the talking adults. Their dim spoons travel from bowl to mouth, bowl to mouth.

'They are certainly grand children,' says Billy Kerr. 'They must get right feeding in the big city. How's that boy today, hah?'

The boy stares out at him, the man who the day before has played with him on the green road. And yet nothing issues forth from him, no easy talk or smile.

'You see,' says Billy Kerr, 'a night of sleep passes, and they forget you.'

'He's only a little fellow,' I say, by way of explanation and perhaps a hint of apology. Because the boy can be oddly silent even with me. You need to tickle him out, like a spider having his web tickled with a stick. The girl is like a secret all to herself, like seven magpies. Five for silver, six for gold. Seven is a secret never to be told.

He's only a little fellow. A little fellow has a memory worthy of remark. He seems to forget and yet another time he can call forth a matter in all its bright details. He chooses to remember in his own good time, cannot remember unless something in him wants to. Not wanting to remember for the boy is the same as forgetting. Perhaps that is what forgetting is, and I would do well to practise that art. The ease and dance of a boy's mind, the rightness of it. But I must think also how easy it would be to destroy his dance, his ease. So I must think well of his father, with that red beard, who as a boy himself had the temper of a wolf — silence, silence, and then the growl and the snap, a ravening temper he could bring to bear on his younger brother. His older brother was different, employing much more elaborate methods of torture. They were a threesome of endless and unnecessary war. And I stood among them not as a mother, which should have been Maud's job, though Maud either doted on or ignored them, and finally, abandoned them and all daily matters, and put herself to bed one autumn morning and never arose again in any purposeful way. There was a horror and a terror in that for the boys, and in chief for the father of this little scrap, who worshipped the ground his mother trod on. The trouble was, she did not issue forth, to trod!

I do believe the little boy never met his grandmother Maud, or perhaps he crossed her time of dying with earliest babyhood.

Certainly Matt worships in turn his little grandson, says he will put him to being a painter like himself, and glories in the prospect. Matt may profess a great disappointment in his eldest son, who he calls a Bohemian, meaning a mere layabout, even though he went himself to be a sculptor in the art college in Dublin. But of this boy's father he never says but good, and of this boy likewise.

The boy again in turn worships Matt, because Matt, when they lived near him in Donnybrook, was always careful to bring boiled sweets on his bicycle every Sunday, and that is the kind of thing that registers with a child.

Soon now Matt will be down with his paints and easel as the summer matures, and I am hoping he will make the journey from Lathaleer, my cousin's farm where he stays, often, for the boy's sake. For my own part it would give me no grief if I never set eyes on him again, for his cruel actions. One of which is, he will not stay here in Kelsha with us, and indeed we have no space for him, but if he wished we would make up the hag's bed for him, where he could sleep the sleep of the just, with the comfort of the sleeping fire. And it would be nothing for us to include his shirts and drawers in the wash, items I knew well in the old fled days when I washed for all those men, him and his three sons. When they were my care.

But the boy is a complete boy, no roaring or beating has pulled the crystal jewel from his crown of contentment. So I must also say a word in favour of his mother, who I know, because it is writ plain in her face, has a dislike for me. Although it suited her to leave the children with us, while they fix their tent in London, I feel she has no great opinion of our abilities. She wrote me a letter of preparation and thanks that reeked of doubt. Luckily she is a rather indifferent mother — the children's clothes were all entirely sent down to me without ironing, and holes in the heels of socks, and tears in trousers left to the mercies of the wind like neglected houses — or I might never have got my mitts on the boy and girl. As Billy Kerr luxuriates in the peace of our kitchen, I am buffeted, tormented even, again by this feeling I have for them. It is like the treacle in the pudding when it is first thrown down on the dough, and the spoon so slow and held back as the mixture is stirred, dragging on the muscles at the top of the working arm. And then the treacle begins to let itself be folded in, and surrenders, and imparts to the pudding that wild taste of sugar, foaming and cavorting in the mouth. Not that treacle pudding features much down here in Kelsha — that was an item of my mother's in the old kitchen in Dublin Castle in our heyday, so the memory of the weak arm is my arm as a little girl helping her mother, in the eternal security of early years.

Chapter Five

'So I am thinking,' says Billy Kerr, 'that pony now, I am sure you will be eager to sell him now, and in that regard I've been asking about Kiltegan and Feddin, and I think I have a man will take him from you, despite the new savagery in him. Because I think he must be a man's pony now, someone that can handle him and put manners back on him. Although I would advocate the gentle touch now with an animal, there must be that hidden strength there in the arm if needed. By God, if a pony wished, he might break everything in his world, with those hooves. He might start to kick and kick till all was sundered and in a thousand pieces. Think of that!'

He has said this in the direction of the children, wide-eyed in their niche. The boy looks to me for confirmation, he licks once at his lower lip. I shake my head in a wordless denial. But I suppose it is true. Nevertheless, I have again that unpleasant but informative creeping in the back of my head, that stirring there like woodlice in a seeming solid log, that doesn't concur with what Billy Kerr is saying, doesn't like it and doesn't know exactly why. But the why is coming close behind.

'And I'd say, you'd be lucky now to get a ten-bob note for that animal, but I think I could get that for you, indeed and I do.'

Ten bob? One nice paper note for such a handsome horse, that Sarah Cullen paid as I remember six pounds, seventeen shillings, and sixpence for, the sixpence returned to her as luck money by the tinker that sold her the horse, and tried to put the spit he spat into his hand into her hand for good measure, and Sarah had to shake on it, as custom demanded, though she is as fastidious as a cat.

'You did us a good turn yesterday, Billy Kerr,' I say. 'And I want to say this with all politeness. But to my mind when a transaction that concerns ready money is to be discussed, you might wait for the other person to open the discussion. Now that's just my way of thinking, dating from the days of my father, when money was a subject that got greater airing. I don't mean to offend you.'

'Heavens above, Annie Dunne, I am not offended. I am only trying to put my way in to help. There'd be nothing for me in a deal like that, except the shilling of the price for my trouble. That's it then. I will bring a man up to look at the animal, and bring the animal down to the man if needs be, and drove it ten miles out the Baltinglass road if necessary. I will bring him to Carlow for you, if the need arises. I am solicitous on your behalf. I only intend to assist you both.'

But he is abashed also, this assisting man. He has flushed up around his sideburns, poor scraggy streals of hair though they be. I have an interesting effect on this man. I am thinking sincere politeness without sincerity might be a better weapon against him, if weapon be required again. But I must bear in mind his epic efforts of the great mishap on the road, I must, I must. It is becoming too easy to discommode this man.

I am looking now at Sarah, standing, looming at the top of the room between the dull shine of her delf and the dull fire of the turf. It is hard to read her face in the gloom, the white hair pulled back from it, her mouth with its little twist in the lips as always. But I can hear, almost feel, her brain thinking. Oh, oh, she loves that pony Billy, because she has great pride in him, and in the shining light brown wood of the trap, and in the glory of the high lamps.

She loves that pony in the half-lights of an autumn evening, when she can clatter along the main road of Kiltegan, the big metal rims of the wheels calling out the music of her triumph in the world, the triumph of her thirty acres and the strange but palpable dominion of the trap. Never married, too crooked in the face, she will say, to marry, but I say too crooked in the head, what with her mass of dreams and her suffering silence, her awkwardness and her oddity — never married, but got this little hill farm of Kelsha in the happy run of things, the dowry of her own mother in the old days. When Billy Kerr speaks of selling a pony, there are many other matters attached in a long necklace of importance and scripture, the very scripture that keeps Sarah happy on her hill and her mind in general a passable human mind, and not a mind to languish in the county home, as my own father's mind once did, because the meanings and musics of his own world were torn away from him and he could not find a singing to answer that pain and change.

Sarah stands in the glooms like some old queen of old, some old monarch of France before the changes maybe. The tide of her own unimportant history laps at her sturdy brogues. Go back, go back, she cries to the hens in the yard at eventide, even as she advances to feed them, go back, go back, like King Canute to the very waves.

'I think I would find it hard to part with Billy,' she says, in the little voice of a cowed child. And in that instance of childish sounds, the little girl breaks from the niche and flies across the flagstones of the floor and almost hurts Sarah by the bang into her knees. Sarah's long sturdy legs are covered in the fresh linens of her yard-dress, she barely notices the affectionate girl, or seems to. Yet a long arm with a long-fingered hand drifts down and touches the head of the little girl, her brown hair in a cow pat of curls, that I must brush before the day is any older. Sarah's face floats there like a window with a stretch of wood nailed over it to keep the weather out, its brightness blighted, interfered with. It is a greater thing even than I thought, the question of Billy. She has the severe bereaved look of a person at a graveside, the rinse-through in the skin a mourner gets, like the influenza, staring to the middle distance as if into the realms of death itself.

'I think I would,' she says. 'Is that all the worth he has now? Ten bob? He's only four year old.'

'No,' I say. 'He must be seven now, at least.'

'Is he seven?' she says. 'Even so, a cob like that has years in him. And how could I sell him? I would have to look at him in another man's field as I pass by, and not have the feeding of him, and the talking.'

'The talking?' says Billy Kerr.

So I carry him on from there.

'The talking about him, she means,' I say, 'with me, in the evenings. He has provided many stories up here on the hill, hasn't he, Sarah?'

'He has. But he also has his way of talking,' says Sarah. 'The scuttering and the slithering of his lips, and when he doesn't like a thing, he'll tell you.'

'That's right,' says the boy at the fireside. 'He speaks Irish.'

'Ah well,' says Billy Kerr. 'Look, it's only . . .'

Then a rare thing happens. Sarah's high head dips down, her frosty perm shows its crown, and light enough hair it is now, not the growth of old as dense as bog cotton. You can see the fine pink skin of her inner head. I know what she is doing. Just the odd time you will see it. The little girl knows too, because she can feel the small shudders in Sarah's legs, coming down from her eyes and face bones. Sarah's tears. She cries as elegant now as a film star, without much noise. There's more than Billy the pony in those tears, that silver deluge that marks her rough cheeks. There's other things, the tolling bells of other matters, the arrangement of little things that afflict us all, and give strength and engine to our tears, whenever they should fall. They are the tears of an ageing woman without a mate, I must surmise. But whether Billy Kerr could know this is another matter. Men know nothing but their own bellies, and if there is space for their feet they think all is well.

So I am helping her drive the two milch cows back up onto the upper garden for pasture, the children like two wheeling creatures themselves, delighted to be going out on such a great adventure. Billy Kerr is only an aftertaste in the mouth now, bitter, puzzling. Sarah's bony face carries a small cloud. I wonder what she is thinking. I know what she is thinking, I think, but I wonder what it is all the same.

The ground is hardening nicely after a spring of teeming rain, and the horny feet of our cows barely leave a mark, except on the lower ditchy ground where the water congregates and cannot escape. There the two heaving girls drag their legs and their empty udders swing about. They seem to relish the drying ground, and gain a spring in their step when they reach the crustier part of the field. Sarah lays her ashplant lightly across their high rear bones, as a way of conversing them up the slope. There lies the rising sea of soft green grasses. We feel the same delight to view it as those cows, Sarah and me. We feel it as a compliment, as a blessing, or I do. Sarah's cloud this morning stands in her way.

The children throw themselves down on the sloping field and let themselves roll away freely down, and though it tramples the good grasses a little, we are not women to halt the play of children. Daisy and Myrtle will know the trick of tonguing up the fallen grasses. Down the great slope of the field they go, faster and faster, their thin limbs flashing from them like daddy-long-legs, the squeals out of them like the poor pig when I go to cut his throat, or feed him, one or the other. I laugh and look to Sarah, and even with her cloud she smiles.

'Will you latch the high gate,' I say, 'and we can leave these girls to their work?'

'There's poor Furlong in the wood,' says

Sarah, and I catch also a glimpse of the rabbit man, damply creeping through the damp mosses of the trees, not looking at us, no doubt, but keeping his eyes on the ground with its coats of pine needles, for the little nooses he will have left for those rabbits. He is a sad man enough. His brother had a dark head, and one night in a fit of strange temper he killed their mother, when Jack Furlong was about twelve and asleep in his bed.

They had a house there below Kelsha, one of the old mud-walled jobs, that has long disappeared back into its garden of fuchsia and orange lilies that the mother herself had planted in her first days of marriage, as women do in their gardens, all full of hope. The father was a will-less man that went every year to Scotland for the harvests there, and one year never returned, but is supposed to have married a Scottish girl bigamously and lived happily ever after. Jack's brother was a quiet, strong lad that worked on the roads for the council, and he slew his mother with a pickaxe, driving the blunt point in between her shoulder bones as she lay sleeping. Then he dragged her out in the dark and dug a neat ditch, and buried her in under a fuchsia bush all in red bloom.

So they took him to the madhouse in Carlow, and buried the mother, and Jack was left, and he is strange enough himself, but gentle and polite. He has a face like a hunting dog, with heavy whiskers, and he knows only the one song, a favourite of my own, 'Weile Wáile', and this one song he sings continually, and I don't know how the rabbits don't mind it, but he catches enough of them. Sometimes you will go into a house and see on the dresser the ears of a rabbit, neat and dry, and on the fire smell the pot of stew boiling, and know that Jack Furlong has been by and made a sale of a stringy rabbit for a couple of eggs, or a wrap of butter.

His little song drifts down over the spent heathers,

> *'There was an ould woman and*
>   *she lived in the woods,*
> *Weile, weile, wáile,*
> *There was an ould woman*
>   *and she lived in the woods,*
> *Down by the river Sáile.'*

And late in the summer every year the mother's lilies still bloom.

'There he is,' I say.

'I suppose the children wouldn't like

rabbit for their tea?' she says.

'I don't know, why not? They're as good as rabbits there anyhow, rolling down the field!'

'Heya, Jack, Jack Furlong!' she calls. 'Have you ever a rabbit for us?'

Well, he stops in the murk of the trees, as startled as a deer. No doubt he was deep, deep in his thoughts. Oh, what thoughts might they be? Does he go over and over the dark history of his people? His long loneliness and neglect, the loss of all, his father vanished, his brother under lock and key in Carlow? No doubt, no doubt. He stops in the dresses of the pine trees, with their sharp hoops, and stares out from the dark at us, two old women with two milch cows in the bright sunlight of the summer. And a darkness passes from his face, and he raises a hand like a proper countryman, and what is that look in his face? Only lightness, the lightness of gratitude.

Sarah goes up the field then and goes as far as the brambles of the low hill-wall, and Jack the same the other side, and without a proper word he hands a dangling snag of a thing across the loose stones with a strong arm, and Sarah lifts her own strong arm and he gives the rabbit over into her care, he letting go of his grip on the ears, she taking the grey creature by the long soft paws.

Sarah comes back to me.

'I don't know what that means,' she says.

'What what means?' I say sharply. 'Did he say something to you?'

'I said I would give him two of your fine brown eggs for it, and he says, "No, Sarah Cullen, have grace of it." Now what does that mean, have grace of it?'

'It isn't the King's English anyway.'

'It isn't even Kelsha English,' she says, laughing her laugh.

And when we look again to spy him and his mysterious English, he is gone among the trees.

'Auntie Anne, Auntie Anne, look at us, look at us!'

The girl and boy have locked themselves in a fast embrace and are throttling each other without regret, as they speed in a double heap down the raging field.

'Do you think,' says Sarah, though barely to me, mostly to the quiet countryside about, 'that there will be life much after that pony? Do you think it will be worth living at all?'

This is a very big question and I am not qualified to answer, not entirely. I look down at the rich grasses. All sorts of insects happily resort there, a shiny black beetle heaves himself along a dipping blade.

'Do you not feel,' she says, 'the wind of change? It is like the Bible sometimes up here, living here. We are like the Jews of old. It shakes me, the talk of Billy Kerr. He speaks like my father, all sense and certainty. There's safety in that man, and still he shakes me.'

This is a large speech for Sarah, and which I don't understand. She has spoken with ease and surety, very definitely, like marking cloth before cutting, straight and confident as such marks must be. Many months can go by, especially in the winter, when Sarah will say nothing beyond the usual round of instructions, agreements and ordinary observations. Then suddenly, a pronouncement as dark and uncomfortable as a sibyl.

'There is nothing,' she says, 'that anyone could say would dissuade me, dissuade me from the opinion that.'

'That what?' I say, beginning to be rightly frightened.

'Grass stains,' she says.

'What?'

'Grass stains, grass stains, elbows and trouser knees, think of the scrubbing and rubbing in that.'

'I do not follow you at all, Sarah,' I say.

'The children,' she says, 'the children and their rolling.'

'That fierce master, Tommy Byrne, taught us all the epics.'

It is Sarah talking, by the fire, hardly heeding us her listeners, if talking it really is. It might also be said to be a kind of old singing. Things she likes to say, over and over.

'He beat us without mercy when we were small and spindly. But he had a terrible appetite for the Roman poets, and we learned of the doings of Aeneas in the early days of the Romans. Virgil it was wrote that. And he said we could learn anything we would ever need to know about farming from Virgil, in his book, the Eclogues. And do you know, Annie, the curious thing was, we knew nearly everything that Virgil had to say, even as the master read it, about tilling and sowing and harvesting, because we had been looking at it from the days our eyes first opened at our mother's breasts.'

I am washing the two children one by one in the big enamel basin. I have it set out in front of the fire and I am also imploring the boy, whose turn it is now, not to do his favourite swimming motion when my back is turned to fetch an item. He holds the sides of the old curving basin and whooshes himself along through the water, he cannot help it, with the delight of it, and then of course the wave rises up behind him and swamps the great flagstone of the hearth, and he menaces the fire itself with his flood.

But Sarah is in her chair staring off into the middle distance where the light of the oil lamp barely reaches, her face yellowing in the soft light like a stone in the late sun, talking away as softly as the light of other days, when she was young. For myself I went to the Loreto Convent in North Great George's Street in Dublin when my father was head of the castle police, and when he was but a village inspector, to the little school in Dalkey Village, among the wild children of Dalkey, so my memories are not of the little village school in Kiltegan.

Her thoughts — as I soap the boy fiercely, to try and restore him a little to his city cleanliness, not entirely succeeding — have passed easily from a discussion of Billy Kerr ('Billy Kerr shakes me,' she has said again), to the Dunnes of Feddin, to

Winnie Dunne, who is the schoolmistress now in Kiltegan, to her own schooling there, and the master Byrne, who died of peritonitis in the thirties sometime. He was one of those old-time teachers seemingly with nothing but the classics between himself and ruination. His own father had been the keeper of a proper hedge school, where the penniless classes of Catholics and Protestants went for their education. They weren't real hedges, but poor bad sorts of buildings going begging, lean-tos and the like, the sort of crazy habitation that might suit a labourer and his offspring till the very roof fell in on them.

I don't know what it is about Sarah these times, but some little latch has been loosened in her tongue, by something, by someone. She is very much a brighter person and the usual glooms have been lifted out of her, and she is engrossed now in remembering. Even the boy listens to her like a robin with its head at a listening angle, another sort of latch. It is how a robin looks at me in the yard in the winter when I sally forth — as if about to speak to me civilly, as if expecting some small morsel for himself, and why not?

The boy at any rate makes no complaint of my scrubbing, whereas the girl fell quickly into tears of vexation, not at all wanting to be naked, though she is perched now on the hearth seat almost wholly wrapped in a big old sheet I use for drying them, and her own innocent disc of a face is entombing its thoughts in the low gutters of the turf.

'The best days of your life, your school-days,' I say.

'I was at school already,' says the boy. 'We learned Inchworm and Thumbelina. They're songs for singing.'

'That's right,' says the girl dreamily, deeply at her ease, 'we did. Or I learned them and you sort of learned them,' she says to her brother.

'I sort of learned them,' he corrects himself, looking up at me.

'Inchworm,' I say. 'What is an inchworm? How does it go, dear?'

The little girl begins to sing. She has a flat, peculiar little voice for herself, but it is thin and with enough colour to suggest a tune, like a penny whistle or the like. 'Inchworm, Inchworm, measuring the marigolds,' she sings. It is a song I have never heard. They have songs now no one has heard, first-time songs, unlike years ago, when all the songs were known by everyone and a new song was like a wind from the Sahara, bearing a strange red dust, a miracle. The little boy squeals with delight, squirming he is with the pleasure of it, like a proper audience. The girl's face is still, radiant. The boy bangs in the bath, knuckles and other bones finding the enamelled tin. Such is the nature of his delight, turning his little contraption of being into queer drumsticks.

'You and your arithmetic, you'll probably go far . . .'

Outside the heavy hot wind of the summer night stirs the fresh leaves of the sycamore. The moon no doubt will be riding to the south, where it sits above the sloping field. Suddenly, in the byre, Billy will fall asleep, just suddenly there where he stands, his guilt evaporating in slumber, like a human. The calves will curl up on the shitty hay, and breathe heavily through their stupid noses like old men with colds. Even the hens will nervously sleep, the night fear of foxes infecting their henny dreams, whatever they might be, I could not say. And we will dry and settle the children in their beds, in their pyjamas aired by the sun on the fuchsia outside, with the good air of Kelsha in the crisp cotton, and they will sleep. And we will go to our bed, and we will sleep. Which seem like good matters.

The water runs down the little boy's back. I am using an old ladle of my grandmother's, the last of the stewards' wives. Her house at the back of Kiltegan village had a whole arsenal of kitchen items — she could have gone to war with them — and her array of skillets and pots astounded less fortunate eyes. Now what remains of all that glitter and show is this tarnished ladle, made by Mellet's of Baltinglass.

Where the rest of her worldly hoard has gone I cannot hazard a guess. But the ladle was with us at the castle quarters, so it must have been a keepsake of my father's, in memory of her. Now all my mother's things are dispersed also, and only this ladle has come from that time, passing through two or three sets of women's hands. It scoops the bath water well enough, the little boy's back glistens at me, with its slender spine, his skin as soft as gloves. I think of my grandmother, Bridget Dunne, and him, the past and the present. Her long set of bones lie in against the church in Kiltegan yard, his fidget below me.

Chapter Six

The weather turns filthy in the deeper part of the month and the wind whips about in the yard for three curious days. I am always surprised by our weather, even though there is nothing surprising about it. There is no mystery. It will not hold. The summer months seem always to be thinking and dreaming of winter and now and then those thoughts and dreams break out into waking reality. And the signs and sounds of winter are laid across the good colours of summer, the green of the sycamores darkens, the brown mottled bark deepens to black in the wet. Even a few leaves are torn from the branches in an imitation of autumn, and those fresh soft leaves that should have lasted many weeks more lie suddenly at sea on the stones of the yard and on the soft, high summer grasses. Bewildered and disgruntled I do not doubt, like people in their prime torn from life, and chicks pulled out of the nest.

So we retreat into the familiar darkness of the kitchen. And perhaps it is not like the lows of winter in that we do not expect such weather to last, and we have the sunlight to anticipate. And moreover the rain is not driven in under the doors and eaves, and down the chimney. We do not come out in the morning to find a drift of snow advancing on the very ashes of the fire, two very different heaps of white. The walls do not weep for the horrors of winter, the mattresses do not gain that miserable odour of damp that only a few hours under the covers expels by the heat in your body. Otherwise there are echoes and odours of winter enough in that bad summer weather, a memory and a prophecy.

This is when the bond of friendship between me and Sarah is most essential, when it is tested and I do pray strengthened by confinement, and the little necessary dances and manoeuvrings on the flags of the kitchen floor.

Of course we must be perpetually butting out into the drives of rain and wind, to accomplish the usual roster of chores. Nothing stops the great clock of the day, with its silent bells ringing the changes in our heads — cows, calves, hens and all. We throw on our old torn and age-painted coats and push out like ragamuffins into the tempests. We return windblown and a little daft in the head from the buffeting, as if we have had wild dreams while we were abroad. By the hearth the children lurk, drawing on brown paper bags, doing little talking games with their teddy bears, their heads stilling and their eyes widening as the door opens yet again to admit one of us in our tempestuous garb.

So in the deep afternoon of the third day, all work attended to, we are content to be as cooped as the hens. All work attended to, for the most part, except the evening feeding of the hens, not so bad a job as the poor creatures are indeed fast in their coop so that the breezes out from the Glen of Imail will not eradicate them entirely from the confines of the farm, and blow them away over the trees to Humewood, like wonderful rags. I have my old wooden orange box of socks and stockings, to be darning the heels and the toes, where Sarah's horny nails make holes. Sarah herself is banging a lump of dough on the counter of the dresser, shaking fresh white flour under it so it will not stick to the waxen wood, banging, kneading with her bony knuckles, and banging. The boy and the girl turn the thick pages of a book, looking at the simple colours of the figures, absorbed, like priests doing those silent prayers by the tabernacle, things no doubt the mass-goers need not or ought not hear. It is a simple moment, all labour done, the natural anxieties of being alive all stilled and soothed. The turf fire mutters in the murky hearth. The clock seems less anxious to seek the future, its tick more content, slower. All is in the balance of a kind, the weight and the butter in the scales in sufficient harmony.

Then we begin to hear them. At the first distant inklings of sound, a sound that is a sort of memory, something on the tip of the tongue, but that slowly comes back to you what it is, Sarah's head turns and looks across at me. She leaves the dough subsiding on the dresser top. Her floury hands go to her thighs and she rests them there, imprinting the soft map of her palms. We have a moment of inaction and then we both spring to the centre of the floor.

'Do you think, do you think they'll come in?' she says, with real fear in her voice.

'Look out the top of the door,' I say. 'Look out and see!'

We move quick to the door, the children rushing after us, infected by our tones. Sarah unlatches the half-door and looks out through the veritable cloths of the wind, the air is so blustery and torn about. The children shove up on tiptoe and grasp the worn wood and jump up and down to see out as best a child might, who always has half a view, I suppose, of everything. There, down the lane a bit, we start to see them, the wild heads of hair, the laughter and the rags and the wicked faces.

'Are they the crowd came last year?' I say.

'How could you tell?' says Sarah. 'They're a whole tribe are just the same, every one.'

'Their heads are on fire,' says the little boy.

'On fire,' I say, 'on fire?' fully believing that indeed they might be. But it is only wildness afflicts those heads. The rising hanks of uncut hair, dark brown and fair and black, must look like flames to a child.

'We must hold down the latch,' says Sarah, 'hold it down, and say nothing, and not be here!'

'They will know we are here,' I say. 'And we must be here anyway, for the pony, for all the knick-knacks and bits of the yard.'

'I don't care, I don't care. They must not get in to us. Not with the children, not with just ourselves to fend for ourselves.' Then she takes a last glance out and seems to know them after all, and bangs the door shut again. 'That's Mick Brady's crowd of wild-haired kin that are supposed to have roughed over the Flanagan brothers last year, looking for Michael Flanagan's money that they thought was under their mattress, and it wasn't there, because Michael put it in the post office at last at the behest of his brother, and that enraged them, and poor Tom put through the mill, and beaten in his own chair!'

All this hissing from Sarah like the kettle finally topping off, by heavens, and when I glance down now at the boy's face it is twice as wide as the morning, and the girl holding on to one of Sarah's strong legs like a monkey, and she is going, 'Ah, ah, ah,' in a tiny voice.

'Hold down the latch, hold it down,' says the boy, queerly taking charge a moment, all four years him, like a proper man, I suppose.

'I am holding it, I am,' says Sarah, and she is, with all her strength, and her famous arms, that have thrown more hen food than a great barn could hold, and put up three yards of a dry-stone wall in a day, like a man. She leans down on the latch fit to crack it. 'And shush now, all ye, shush, shush.'

So we wait, the four of us, in the great hush, two old women and two scraplings. We are waiting and waiting. Heavily the old clock tock-tocks in the dresser, it is a clock in fact without a tick to its name, only that old banging tock tock. Perhaps it was cheaper bought without the tick. Clocks for sale, clocks for sale, reduced price, owing to the lack of a tick. Oh, but Mick Brady's kind of fierce, wild folk must be creeping quiet themselves up the yard, thinking, are they all away out in this weather, visiting maybe, or braving the wind down to the town? — and judging how likely that would be. Isn't it a day for settled folk to be feeding the fire with turf and holding to the kitchens of Kelsha? And must be smelling the possibilities, tasting them on the fresh wind, what would be missed if they took it, what might they be having the law on themselves for taking, and what could they take that we would only curse them for it, and not be going down to Kiltegan to get Sergeant Collins to look into the matter? Sergeant Collins that suffers so deeply from what is called the black dog, just like my own father years ago. Sergeant Collins who sometimes is so afflicted with fear and misery that his two brothers have to sit with him in the station house and talk to him of matters long ago, when they were all children, and then the sergeant gets the feet of himself again, and starts to laugh, and is as right as rain then for a bit, and sees to his duties with great respect and diligence. What ruined the sergeant is the great education he had off the people in Maynooth, when he went first to be a priest, but never got out of his civilian clothes in the upshot, but spent two great years reading whatever they give to young men to read to make them priests, and all that mythology and theology just made him habitually sad. It leaves oftentimes the district without a guardian, though for myself I would accept such a situation for the sake of the sergeant, in memory of my father. Still and all, now, sergeant, rise up, rise up, and give your horse some hay. We wait, we wait, Sarah a-tremble on the latch, the dull gleams of the stormy day flitching in through the gaps in the door, the silence not a real silence, but a roar of anticipation.

The old green flagstones are under us. They are our anchor. And then suddenly there is a hand outside on the latch, because it is shoved down and almost goes up through Sarah's hand inside, as if a great fish were attached to it, and it a sort of hook. Sarah lets out air through her lips and teeth, teeming with the effort, her bad-sighted eyes staring with the fright, glancing at me for courage, and I give her back the glance with as much of that as I can muster. The little boy lets out a minuscule cry and then throws a hand over his mouth like an actor, gulping. Down Sarah's dress suddenly appears a dark stain, flooding out from her private place, it is a terrible thing. The wild tinkers rattle on the latch, rattle and rattle.

We can hear their low dark gabble outside, their rough words, the gruff hisses of the women, the laughing anger of the men. Who are these people? Some say they are the remnants of wars, ragged soldiers and their kin returning from forgotten battlefields, who never reached home, or whose homes were razed before them, over a hundred years ago. My father opined they were the last of the lost people in Ireland without farm or shelter, or were people so close to nature they wished like birds and badgers to be bedding down under scrappy hawthorns and the like, with their coverings of old mended canvas like a concession thrown to human ways. They are not all wild like this, there is the Dempsey tinkers that mend your pots and buckets and one of the Dempseys took up with a travelling forge for all the horses and ponies of this part of Wicklow and became nearly respectable, till he was killed stone dead by a stallion, when he touched the fire by accident against the animal's skin. But there is a grievous hatred and fear of such as these ragamuffins beyond the door, laughing at our terror, rattling the latch. They would not have come into my grandfather's yard in such a manner, the old steward of Humewood, they'd have hung at the back door of the steward's house, hoping for an old hat or a scrap of soup from the pot on the ancient stove. Maybe they are pulling in against us now because they believe we are fallen from our great perch, and it makes them merry in themselves to feel the power of fright they have over us. Or maybe no such thought crosses their minds, grown across with brambles and bog cotton and rushes as those minds must be.

And what they would do if they get in I do not know. Will they tear the clothes off our old backs, and beat us stripped across the yard with hazel wands, as once happened to an old fellow living alone in the deeps of Imail, because he refused these wild boyos and girleens an ounce of sugar for their billycan? Will they chance to speak to us? Will they enter like a storm and then be civil? It seems to impart them endless amusement now to grip the latch and drive it down, because they know well there is a hand on it the other side. The murk of the darkened daylight hangs in the room. It is they who own the stormy sunlight outside. They feel the whips of the wind, we the wandering threads of the heat of the fire. It is two different worlds, and they wish to sunder the veil between them, this old blue door thrown together from planks.

'Throw up your own hands on my own, do please, Annie,' says Sarah. 'I am getting very tired.' And I am just doing that when the pressure goes off the latch suddenly, and there's the silence again, utter silence. We grip our bones tight inside that silence, and I have a vision of them all outside, between our two windows with the pots of geraniums, their faces quiet, and staring, and waiting, grinning before the prospect of some further mischief. It is a terrifying vision.

At length I put an eye to the crack in the half-door and peer out. Only the empty spaces of the yard greet my gaze. I strain my face in against the wood to try and get a sight to extreme right and left. Only the hapless storm buffets about in a lonely fashion, rattling a bucket over by the milking shed, shaking out the old harnesses of the branches of the maples. For I think sometimes the maples are like horses brought in together to have the big ploughing harnesses thrown across them, in the time of ploughing, their bark strangely polished like the heavy polish of the leather bands of harness, and even in the secretive world of the cargo of their leaves there are gleams, like the gleams of brass and emblems.

Grind up the furze-roots, and bring them to the sycamores, so they may plough the mucky winds! Poor horses are new men with the furze. Poor Billy could be put to plough, and is, as long as he gets the furze. A neighbour's horse will help the day, but beware, beware, you have to give them both the furze, or one will not pull in the traces. Grind up the furze, and bring them to the sycamores!

There is not a soul, tinker or farmer, in the yard that I can see. The gap of the gate is empty, only a few fresh leaves torn from their summer perches tumble and stick on the wet green road. It is strange and quiet, very strange and quiet, as if we have woken from one dream to the next, and nothing to join them except the sudden start of waking.

We go out now like soldiers after siege to view our invaded quarters. While some were rattling the latch, others were strolling through the offices of the yard, laughing no doubt, exultant, victorious. Sarah's face is long and silent, troubled. Her white hair looks like it might crackle if you touched it. There is something in that face that makes me more fearful than the fear of the tinkers. It speaks volumes, but I do not know what is written in them. I must ponder it, ponder it all, this too now on top of all the other mysteries. Suddenly I feel unmoored, a sway of disquiet occupies some little quarters behind the eyes.

As forfeit of their victory over us they have taken a coil of rope from the doorway of Billy's dark byre, where it hung on a rusty iron bar, an ordinary rope used as Billy's halter, if halter were needed in a hurry, not an uncommon thing with Billy. A length of old rope bearing the presses and stains of a curmudgeonly pony. Nothing else that we can see, unless the tincture of daily happiness that we were engaged in is something that can be taken off like a veritable rope up the wild, leafy road towards Keadeen.

Now we will be the stuff of jokes around their campfire tonight, wherever they alight before the coming of the summer dark.

Sarah betakes herself into the bedroom with her soaked clothes. I say nothing about that accident, and she has entered her fold of silence like a star accused by the dawn light. I know she is shaken, and ashamed. It is often a woman that has given birth to children that has trouble with her bladder, but Sarah has had no adventures of that sort. It will be only fear and age. The years return us gradually to the afflictions and shames of childhood, it is a curiosity of existence. For her I do feel. For that old woman Mary Callan beyond in her damp field and damper cabin I feel only too little. For Sarah I do feel.

'It's not something I can say, to say about it,' I begin, later that day. We have performed the rest of our tasks with the perfect solemnity of Benedictine nuns under a vow of silence. She is folding her clothes into her drawer, over by the unhelpful light of the oil lamp. Even from my niche in the big bed I can smell the camphor bags she has tailed in there, against the appetites of the moths. I have covered the last turves over with turf ashes, so they will burn as slow as snails all night, and in the morning I will rake off the ashes and they will be as red as best coals, and give me fire quickly all over again in the sunless crispness of six o'clock. No morning comes but that I think of our quarters in Dublin Castle, the beautiful fireplaces there, far too grand, my father used to say, for a chief superintendent of modest outlook, but to me and my sisters the marble had almost a quality of singing. It sang to us of the future, of promises, of love. By such fires would duly come, we believed, good officers of the garrison, low and junior ones of course, but more than welcome with their English accents and their burning eyes. For we could conceive then of no young man that had not burning eyes, like in the stories we adored. We were the offspring of a Wicklow rook, a big, wide man like a stone-fronted barn, but those fireplaces made brief swans of us. And because we had the use of the castle coals, we set those fires with coals every winter's day, and sat on our delicate battered furniture out of stores, and were proper little girls, whose mam was dead. When on appointed days the Viceroy swept in in his carriages, and we heard great levies going on, their wonderful noises filtering though buildings and yards to us like true floating stories themselves, that sea of sound struck against us like little shores, and enchanted us.

Days so far off! Not marble fires and foolish dreams now, but Sarah folding her well-darned underclothes, her long woollen stockings, her thick, rough blouse, in a meagre light, in a meagre house.

'Nothing to say about it, indeed,' says Sarah, burdened by despair.

'The change in the weather will work all sorts of mischief with people, see if it does not. You'll be hearing about it all over. There won't be a household now in Kelsha without a medical mishap.'

'Maybe, maybe so,' she says, with solemn simplicity, with sadness, folding the clothes as if it were a ritual, a priestly thing — when the priest used to be 'fussing about', as we thought as children, at the altar, with his back to us, and never a look or a word, and the dread shaft of boredom striking down into our limbs, and us twitching like just-slaughtered calves on the cold benches. Religion was a terrible burden to us as little girls, excepting the excitement after mass, when you could count your cousins alive on the church steps, and dead in the churchyard.

'I wouldn't think twice about it, if it happened to me, I wouldn't now, Sarah.'

'It didn't happen to you, Annie.'

'No, no.'

'If there was a leak in our roof, I would expect a man to go up on the slates and mend it. I would expect a helpful man to bring his ladder and his roof ladder, or knock one up in the yard with a few lengths of timber, and scale the heights there and do what he had to with his hammer and his lead.'

'Oh?' I say.

'And if there was a leak in a bucket, I would want the tinker Dempsey himself to come with his metal and his fire and plug the gap fiercely.'

'We had enough of tinkers for one day, surely.'

'But when there is a leak in an old woman, what is the best thing? To bring up the stun hammer from the slaughterhouse in Hacketstown, and lay it in against her foul, old temple, and give her a good bang with it, and cure her lep for herself.'

I laugh despite myself, under the warming sheets, not at all sure if I might not be giving her offence. But she has humour in her, Sarah. She laughs too.

'And cure her lep for herself! Ha, ha, ha!'

Then she stands quietly with the bowl of the lamplight.

'Wasn't it lovely when we were young girls and we hadn't these things to worry about. You could wet the bed in the long ago and no one say boo to you, except your mamma might be vexed and muttering at the extra work. But the sheets'd go through the storm of washday and everything washed away, stains and troubles, and not a word said about it again.'

'How do you mean, Sarah?'

'I mean, Annie, such things were by the by, and the future was there to set against any to-do and turmoil was going on. Now there is not that. There is too much fear.'

'Fear, Sarah?' I say fearfully.

'Fear, yes. Where has all the days gone? How am I nearly sixty-two next year and the summers gone that were allotted to me, and days and weeks and years all added up to that amount already? Where is all that time? Where is it gone? We were young one day and that tomorrow came and we were no longer young. The Dunnes of Kelsha were young, and you were, and your sisters Maud and Dolly, and of those six girls only the one was wed, and she is dead now.'

'Poor Maud. We thought she had seen paradise. Such a wedding day. She did not look well even that day, but when I saw those babies, one after the other boys — it is sad to be sad on your sister's wedding day. And I suppose, with my crooked . . .' — I am going to say back but I do not say it, I cannot — 'how could I expect, different, no . . .'

'I think in all truth you would have made a fine mother, Annie, and those two little children within certainly have a great liking for you. They run about the place. They seem to break everything, Annie, how is that? I try to see them, to peer into them, but they are like shadows.'

'How is it shadows they are like, Sarah?'

'To remember, just to remember, what it was like, littleness — I barely, scarcely — but you, you have the knack, you have the wrist for children, like for the butter, I could never make happy butter. I can make it, but not happy butter. I understand nothing of it, or of children. They have something ahead of them, and this I no longer understand. The little girl is strange to me, she is strange.'

'Well now, she is a little strange.'

'She is quiet and strange. She looks at me. The little boy talks to me, but she just looks, as if she thinks I am a very odd bird indeed. She has asked me nothing since she came. She does my bidding, one, two, three. But she asks me nothing.'

'They are city children.'

'But you were a city child. You were a city child, Annie, in your heyday. And I envied you that, except, I was happy enough being Winey Cullen's daughter.'

'I wasn't a city child like them. My father carried the country with him. Even in the castle he led a country life. He patrolled the streets of Dublin as a countryman, as a Kiltegan man. His happiness arose from being from somewhere else. Those children are really from Dublin, born in Dublin and knowing only Dublin, till they are sent down here just to put a twist in their heads!'

'And God bless them,' says Sarah. 'God bless us all, God knows.'

She takes her leave of her folding and steps the few paces of the boards to the bedside and kneels down with her long bones and prays into her large hands, her big horse's face buried in the callused fingers. She has thin layers of yellow skin on the working sides of her hands, that no pumice stone will erase. You cannot run out Sarah's hands with a pumice, though she attempts it daily. And she rubs in lavender water, and she sprinkles it all over her body now and then, to freshen herself, she says. You cannot leave good linen in a damp box, she says. You cannot keep a book far from the fire, or it rots, she says. Lavender water, Sarah's idea of youthfulness. She grows it up under the woods like a secret, and when it flowers she gathers them and dries them, and when they are well dry she steeps the flowers in warm water to gather out their smells, and she puts the scented water into an earthenware bottle that her mother kept for the same purpose. Maybe her grandmother also smelled of lavender, I do not know. Her prayers done, she creaks into bed beside me.

'Oh, but, it is good to lie down,' says Sarah, 'it is good.'

'It is good,' I say.

Sarah breathes out, her lavender is in her breath.

'In the moment of rest there is safety,' she says. 'There is riches.'

'I think so,' I say.

'No matter what, no matter what fears afflict us, we have our own dry bed to lie in, and we talk to each other like Christians.'

'And that's right,' I say.

'And those wild tinkers are gone away now another while, and God bless the poor people under Keadeen.'

'God bless them.'

'Joseph Casey and his brother Jem, and Katherine Keady that lives alone just under the dip of the hill. God protect them.'

'Amen,' I say. 'Amen.'

There is nothing then for a long, long time, except the slip of wind in the maples outside.

'And Annie,' she says suddenly, but in that ease of starch and cotton, 'was there really a sailor that wanted you?'

'What's that, Sarah? What put that into your head?'

'I hardly know. I was thinking of the folding of the clothes, what ease it gives, and the folding and unfolding of the sea where the Liffey meets it, at the Great South Wall where once your brother-in-law Matt took me walking, one time I was in Dublin for to have my eyes seen to. I don't know why I was thinking of that at all, but those long gold waves and the severe dark river, folding and folding one into the other, and then I was thinking of all those docklands that Matt loves to paint on his lunch-times, or so he said, and I have seen some of those pictured, well, and then I was thinking of sailors in their salty ships, you know, and then I was thinking of you, and what Maud told me once, long long before she took to her bed, in the days when she was always full of funny stories — she was sad but the stories were always humorous, you know?'

'And what did she say about me?'

'She was saying that you at one time was asked to be going off with a sailor, a sailor that came ashore at the boatyard in Ringsend to mend his keel, and he met you, I do not know where, and asked you to walk out with him, and then he went away, and you were waiting, waiting and waiting for him to come back and have that walk with you, that it was to Buenos Aires you thought he had gone, which is a long way enough.'

I lie there awhile beside her. I don't know what the truth is. One day on the big yellow stones of the docks I was walking and a sailor leaned out from his dirty cargo ship and asked me for a kiss. I did not even answer him, but passed on without a glance. Or maybe this memory was at first made up, at this distance I no longer know rightly. When I got back to our quarters in the castle I told Maud something of the kind, and embellished the story, I am sure, in the telling. Because I did not want her to be thinking it was always Dolly and her got the interest, and there might be a man in the end who might overlook my damnable hump and take the risk of loving me. Then that shadowy man became my sailor, and Maud often told her friends of my sailor, maybe even to bolster herself as well as me against this crookedy back. Till I came to believe in him myself, and lived many a year by him, and waited for him, and am maybe waiting for him still, even though he was a queer little dark man on a Portuguese tramp steamer amusing himself by saying hello to a humpety girl on an idle Dublin Sunday — unless that is all invented too. A foolish, dark old woman, me!

'Aye, there was a sailor once,' I said, 'that I might have taken if I'd had a mind to.'

'You had a better score than me, so,' she says. 'World, one, Sarah Cullen, nil.'

'You oughtn't to mind such a thing.'

'That's what people say to the heartbroken and I heard it often enough. A priest said it to me once, when I wept in his confession box. Suddenly weeping, and him just a young fella out of the seminary, in Hacketstown it was. Father O'Keefe, that hanged himself in forty-seven. "You oughtn't to mind such a thing," he said to me, and hanged himself the following year.'

'I'm sorry, Sarah.'

'Arrah, what can you do?'

I think of my crab-apple tree, alone in the summer dark. I wonder what is its purpose. An apple tree has only a hint of roots but it has stood well enough. I think it gains comfort from the manure heap near by, the heat of it, a strange insurance against frosts. I think that evil weather has passed now, the peace of the summer has returned. Now and then the rare note of the hens sounds, that ripple of clucking they do in their sleep, as if they are dreaming of foxes. I think of all the animals of the night creeping across the darkened fields.

'I am thinking now,' says Sarah, 'of Joe McNulty, that went out one morning with a scythe and scythed a whole acre of wheat, to set a marker, he said, for the next generation. And boys brought buttermilk to him all the livelong day, against the monster of thirst grew in his throat. His huge back swiping and swiping at the standing wheat. At the setting of the sun he threw down that scythe, and flung his whetstone far off into the bog just by him there, and let out a crazy roar. The boys sat up on the ditch and cheered. He was something of a man, and that was the man I wanted for my bed. But he might as well have been the president of America, for all I could get close to him.'

'I always thought there were hundreds of boys trying to get you. You were a lovely long slip of a girl, all wheaten-haired and brown and strong.'

'Hundreds,' she says, and laughing a little.

The mice are afoot too in the ceiling. Sometimes tiny drips of water come down from between the ceiling boards. Can it be they are trying to piss on our heads? I think of the silence of the kitchen with its patient and never-regretting clock, the plates in the dresser with the destroyed light altering the blue and white in their glaze. It must be half ten at night, it is only the early summer, not yet the peculiar long days of light when we draw the curtains to encourage sleep, and the daylight lies in the yard like drying straw. Perhaps I will not sleep tonight, but Sarah sleeps, the old embroidered blanket over her face, its hart and hounds forever caught hunting across the low, unstable hills of her breast. What keeps me awake is a dread, an anxiety, an unease I have no name for. My own breaths are short and sharp, my body cannot obey the commands of sleep. And yet by length of trying, by hook or by crook in the woods of the night, seemingly I do sleep.

Chapter Seven

In the folds of the dark she awakes, Sarah, drawing me up like a dark bucket from the deep well of sleep, hand over hand. I can already feel her agitation when I have not even broken the soft surface of normal wakefulness. In the dropping shadows I can see her. She seems to loom up as far as the wooden boards of the ceiling, although she is merely sitting up in the bed, the old bones of her bottom crushing down into the tight straw of the mattress, the tight ticking, so I am almost rolling over against her. My angle of vision from the pillow enlarges her, expands her, her wild white hair like foam or fire, her nostrils begging air, her long hands beating gently on the coverlet. Maybe she was dreaming darkly under the coverlet, till it became a little hot hell of nightmares, which she is by custom afflicted by. The dark of the room is stirred by her fears, the browns and blacks seem to boil around us, the sticks of furniture themselves caught in the petty maelstrom of her panic, twisted out of their places, crooked side table, the pitcher for water in its hole, rickety chairs to take a throw of clothes but never the weight again of a person, except it was a child, swinging its legs to make the creaks come alive in the damaged wood. The leaves of the sycamores make a green waterfall of the wind, all unseen, beyond the cold glass of the window. The mice no doubt scamper in the rafters gleefully. The two old dames below awake!

Billy Kerr is almost a memory when next he returns. That is the way of the summer. Even to an old woman, time gains again some of the rope and length of early days. We are mired even happily in the sweet weeks of June, when vigour is everywhere, the green of everything violent and hungry, the young brambles anxious and ambitious to cover every neglected dip and awkward hillock of our fields. Perhaps that is the great note of the summer, an awful anxiety that takes itself into everything like a strange rot in the windowsills, eating out the hearts of things till you could put your finger through the last coat of sorrow.

Never mind that the end of such doings is clear even as they begin, even as the grasses tear up from the warming ground, and the brambles throw strong cables across surprising distances, and the first pale green signs of the blackberries burn in the thorny ropes. For a countrywoman, if such I am, knows the end of such ambitions, the berries at last boiling with the wasteful pounds of sugar in the big cooking pot, the white sugar creating lighter veins of reddish streaks, as bitter berry marries to the sweetness of the beet. The grasses devoured by the milch cows, and all those grasses out of reach lying exhausted and sere in the revenges of autumn. All swept away, vanishing by a fierce magic off the old woven carpets of the earth.

The marriage coverlet is woven and embroidered for the happy pair, the house is built in a few summer weeks by the *meitheal* of neighbours, the last twist and stitch is put to the thatch, and in they go, the fortunate couple, with strength and purpose — and at length the house is desolate and empty with only rain for a roof, the stranger comes and opens the rotted hope chest, and puts their fingers to the folded coverlet, which falls from their hand in mouldy fragments. And that's all we can say about it, the shortness, the swiftness, and the strange unimportance of life.

But when June is queen, eternally in the grasses, in the wood pigeons, in the dank rooks, in the potato gardens, in the cabbage patches, wild dreams are given birth to with all the mighty energy of the full-blowing year.

All things and creatures feel it. I am not immune. A strange and inconvenient affection takes a hold of me. I go down beyond the midden to my crab-apple tree and talk to it. Now and then I touch it, like patting a child on the head. I watch its progress carefully, like the mother of the same child. I pinch out whatever the late frosts have done to it, and scrape off the mildew, and every week or so I lime-wash the bottom of the trunk against such insects as like to climb up towards the shoots. I dig and tussle up the soil around its rim, I feed it the tea leaves from our many infusions. When I read the leaves in the cups for Sarah, bringing into her head the dreams of soft futures, I am thinking quietly myself of the crab-apple tree, the nourishment it will get from the makings of such prophecies.

I am at the tree that day when Billy Kerr arrives. He is covered head to foot in a strange painting of what looks like snow-flakes, but it is the blurred splashes and drops of the whitewash that he must have been applying to the house of my cousins. Even the backs of his hands are speckled, his cheeks, his nose. It stops in a line on his forehead where he must have had a paper bag over his remnant hair. Any cuts and scrapes now he has on his hands where the lime has touched will be deep pits in his skin by morning, right down to the bone, if he doesn't wash well. Because the lime eats in the hours after painting with it, in the small hours when you lie in bed dreaming, reminding you of the fact that the bodies of hanged men used to be cast into the lime pits in the prisons, to render them down, to get rid of them, to bring utter destruction. So my father would have described it — 'utter destruction'. For the guilty must not expect mercy from other living men, only God could mend their hurts, or the devil increase them. That was all the mind of my father: retribution, punishment, being lost to the world and never found again. It used to frighten me as a little girl, his certainty and his power, devour me with fright like lime itself, in my cosy iron bed in Dublin Castle.

'You were liming today anyhow,' I say, friendly enough, pleased with the heat in my blue and white apron, the scent of rough starch from it rising up to me.

'I was so late with it. The Dunnes were looking darkly at me. So I set to. Tomorrow or the next day when it dries, if there is no rain, their house will be beaming out like a beacon. They want you to come down for tea-time tomorrow, to bring the city children with you, but not Sarah.'

'Sarah never goes down there.'

'No, but, it's not a feud, is it?'

'No, not a feud. A custom. How they live side by side, these companies of single women.'

'And they are cousins, aren't they?'

'I am cousin to the Dunnes and Sarah is cousin to me.'

'I know, I know. What'll I say? Will I say you'll come down?'

'I will be happy to come down. The children will love the adventure.'

'Where are they this moment? I have a Peggy's-leg for them.'

'I don't know. Somewhere about. I'll bring it to them for you.'

He hands me the stick in its crinkling wrapper and I slip it into my apron pocket like a knife.

'Well, you tend that old apple tree well,' he says.

'I do.'

'It is as well to mind an apple tree.'

'It would perish otherwise.'

'Very likely. And you keep the whole place so well, you and Sarah.'

'We have the measure of it.'

'No need for a fella like me about here,' he says, laughing hugely suddenly.

'Men are not as essential as they think they are,' I say, falling suddenly to humour myself, and smiling at him. Not for the first time I try to think what it might be like to be accounted normal — to be easy and fluent with my fellow human beings. In a dream of community and harmony! Nevertheless I feel unaccountably spied on, as if I were emptying out the chamber pots under the bushes, and he was close by, looking and commenting. It is an eerie feeling, certainly.

'And is Sarah about the yard there?' he says.

'Sarah is about the yard,' I say. 'She is trying to decide which of the old hens she will kill and boil. I am afraid it brings a touch of the Solomons to her. She cannot bring herself easily to impose sentence of death on her old acquaintance.'

'I'll go up to her and help her wring a neck! I have no such qualms.'

'No, I expect not,' I say, as he passes by in his limy boots.

I go in to find the children, now that I have true treasure for them. I pass from the wild glass of the sunlight into the familiar blindness of the kitchen. No sign of Sarah at any household tasks, only the clock continues its measured work, taking away the days, or adding new days, I cannot say. My shoes clack on the blue flags. Over at the fire I place a brace of turves and then hear little giggles from the children's bedroom. Armed with the Peggy's-leg, I go in fearlessly, expecting only to find childish things afoot.

The little girl lies on her bed. She is entirely naked to the world. The usual speckles of sunlight that run like shoals of small fish from the window, after being sorted and darned by the leaves outside, illuminate the strange scene. I am nonplussed, bewildered, lost, dismayed. She lies with her face towards the window and does not see me. The boy is huddled between her legs, his face down near where her body joins at the centre, near that special place that should be foreign to all eyes.

'Do lick it,' she says, in her sweet calm voice, innocent as a rose, truly as innocent.

'It smells of oranges,' he says. 'Like when Mummy peels oranges. And rain it smells of.'

'Give it little licks then,' she says.

Six years old talking to four years old, nearly five! Her brother! His sister! Is this a childhood game? I search in my own murky memories for such as this? Did Dolly, Maud and me disport ourselves so? I do not think so. Now my habitual fear engulfs me, it is like a group of men charging me, knocking me down, stamping on me in the mud. My hands seem to wave about at the ends of their stalks. My eyes are suddenly freezing as if winter were driven against them. The bare little room, this niche of Wicklow, this nowhere place, swims about. There is nothing of gaiety in it. My heart is being leant on. I can feel its rafters start to crack and break.

Quickly, on an inner instinct, I withdraw from the room, and then bang sharply on the door. And scrape the chairs by the fire along the flagstones, and rattle the crocks on the dresser, and shake the drawer with all our knives and forks and pudding spoons. And when I think I have warned them enough, I go in again.

Oh, yes, the two of them, in their clothes now, sitting up on their separate beds, smiling the smile of the cat in *Alice in Wonderland*, false, unhappy little smiles. The Peggy's-leg I drive deeper into my apron. I cannot give it to them now. I must think, though I know I will never comprehend.

Perhaps it is a thing that cannot be understood, and so never to be mentioned. I am glad I did not disturb them. I am grateful not to have to puzzle this out with them, even if that is the measure of a coward. *I would spread my cloak under your feet, if it were only the breadth of a farthing . . .*

'Come along then, and we will go down the green road to Kiltegan, and be buying — I don't know, be buying a Peggy's-leg and having fresh air — and all the rest of it.'

The two fire off their beds, the little boy's truckle bed rattling from the excitement.

'And can I carry your purse, Annie, like I always do?'

'You can carry my purse.'

'But he always carries your purse,' says the girl.

'I have only the one purse. I can't be carving it in two with the bread knife.'

'Annie, tell us what you tell us about the bread knife,' says the little boy as we venture out again into the mercy and normalcy of the sun.

'What do I tell you about it?'

'About how to cut the bread with soft sure strokes, and let the teeth of the knife do the work, and not to lean on the bread, or you get crooked big slices that are no good and put the loaf astray.'

'Did I tell you all that? I don't remember.'

'You did, you did.'

'Well, it's all truth,' I say, sallying forth out the pillars of the gates. Do you think Shep would be roused by our progress? Not at all. He lies as if dead in the oven-hot yard, watching us go with half an eye — the farthing of an eye.

'Oh, yes,' says the boy. 'I told my mother. I instructed her. She was leaning, leaning on the bread with her own bread knife. In the yellow kitchen. And that is a knife my father brought home from a party, that a mad drunk priest tried to stab another man with, and my father took the knife off of him. I instructed her, Auntie Anne, just how you told me.'

'I'm sure she was grateful to me. Hmmm,' I say. 'What do you mean about the priest?'

'He doesn't know,' says the girl. 'He is a parrot, you see. He listens, he hears everything, he remembers everything, songs and stories, what everyone says to everyone else, all the things in the rooms, everything, but, he doesn't know what anything means.'

'I see,' I say. 'No more than myself.

What songs do you know? Do you know "Kevin Barry"?'

'No!'

'It's a song of those rebels. Sometime I'll teach you "Kevin Barry". I'll put you up on a chair in the kitchen and you can sing it for me and Sarah and your sister.'

We walk on. The lush grasses are bent underfoot. It is very still and sweet, with the bees crossing our way with perfect music. The meadows steam in the heat. Everything of the year is well advanced, the shoots of meadowsweet, the stalks of the bell flowers. Soon we will be in the wild garden of mother nature herself. That's what it is. I should ask them about the oranges, the kneeling, the opening of the legs. What could it mean? A mad version of what is meant by marriage. Was it horrible and bad? Was it evil I saw? They are so simple and nice and happy. Or is there some bleak shadow in that girl? Some vein of misery? A change, a change so slight and subtle, something I don't ever remember, her simplicity not the same as before. I must watch the girl. I am inclined only to look at the boy. Maybe she needs my assistance. Now I am failing them, I am walking the green road to Kiltegan and failing them.

I look up the sloping field and there beside the granite pillars of the corn-stand are Sarah and Billy Kerr, distant, seemingly talking, but all lost in silence, in the strange silence made up of the music of the bees, the minute roar of a donkey far away, the dull thrum of heat in woods and fields.

I am thinking of that sailor I made up, when Maud and Dolly had me so tormented, when we were girls. Dolly so neat, so young, so loved, so hunted by young men, Maud so clever to capture Matt one sunny day in Stephen's Green, when he was painting the duck pond. Annoyed him into talk! He said he spoke to her just to get rid of her. He did not succeed in that. And think of all that history after. Between the stitching of the coverlet and the fallen house. No time, no time. And these children's father just a scrap it would seem a day ago, a bright boy running in this very vicinity, not so long after his grandfather was dead. A bird of black hair on his head, a wild happiness in him always as a boy, a love for me as big as Baltinglass.

Because when I was young myself, with my famous hump, in well-starched dress and overblouse, I suppose my sisters were anxious for me. They sensed their own powers, they knew I was doomed to live a single lady. They knew no one would want to risk a tribe of humpy children! Oh, I understand it. Look at that girl with her bent back, my heavens — how does she endure? And because they were unhappy for me, they tormented me, they asked the odd boy of their acquaintance to ask to walk me out. Never! And they tormented me, and when they were done, they tormented me more. Such was their love. And Dolly now in America these eternal years, and Maud in her grave in Glasnevin. I cannot bear it all, I cannot. Lying there alone herself, without the solace of her three sons, the embrace of her Matthew. Matt, Matt! I must take a hold of myself now, I must not think these thoughts. At close of day I invented a sailor, a man I said I met in Dame Street, who loved me on sight, and asked to marry me, and then went down to the docks to board his ship and never came back and was likely lost at sea, maybe in the Antipodes! And I made him so fiercely and so well that after a year or two I came to believe in him, and truth to tell I still do. I seem to see him there, solitary in Dame Street with his sailor's coat, talking to me of love and liking, and distant lands. Though I know he did never exist. And I seem to feel again that tender kiss he gave me as we wandered Dublin, in Pearse Street where the gasworks makes privacy for couples. How soft his rough palm on my cheek, how low he stooped, so tall he was, such honey in his words, deep dark honey in the hive before the keeper brings it out to the sunlight, for the honey is made in darkness! And I forbade my sisters ever to mention love again, for it was gone from me, gone in the tragedy of a shipwreck in the wild Antipodes. Wild nonsense, happy nonsense!

I stop on the green road. I am dizzy. The boy sails on regardless, carrying my purse tightly, held slightly aloft, like a dull lamp. And those few pennies in it, all I have. The sunlight blows against the girl, her dark brown hair knits itself into it, joins it, braids the lovely laces of the sunlight. Youth, life, love, my gentle charges, my care. God protect them. Has he protected them thus far? I am sorely frightened. What sloughs of despond, what pits of darkness have they seen? God enfold them, embrace them, retrieve them, perfect them, restore them. I cannot. All I have is the made-up love of a woman with a hump on her back like half the moon.

Chapter Eight

But the main road, when we meet it, brings composure. My heart lightens, the familiar spread of fields and houses, my cousins' farm to the left, the kingdom of Humewood to the right, works on me like a regular prayer. Now my boots go differently. I am singing 'Weile Wáile', to delight the boy, if my old crow's voice can be said to give delight. But a child is merciful and loves what he loves, for a child's reasons. The boy knows bits of it and if the girl knows, she would never sing it anyway. She listens though, she listens with a smile, enjoying the frightening song.

> *There was an ould woman*
> *   and she lived in the woods,*
> *Weile, weile, wáile,*
> *There was an ould woman*
> *   and she lived in the woods,*
> *Down by the river Sáile.*
>
> *She had a baby three months old,*
> *Weile, weile, wáile,*

She had a baby three months old,
Down by the river Sáile.

She had a penknife long and sharp,
Weile, weile, wáile,
She had a penknife long and sharp,
Down by the river Sáile . . .

The riches of summer, the cargo of greens and bejewelled lights, hangs in the hedges, casual, at ease. The heat drives into everything. The world of Feddin and Kiltegan is crisp and dry. My shoes ring on the new tarred road. The accident with Billy nearabouts is only a memory. The children's smaller legs flash along. Perhaps I have witnessed only a dark topic of childhood, particular to them, closed to the world of grown-ups. This is my hope.

I had only sisters to grow up with, so my knowledge of sister and brother is slight. For my brother Willie died away at the old war in 1917 — June the fourth was the day my father kept for him, though you could not know the day of his death for certain — when everything was otherwise, and Ireland was another Ireland altogether. There have been other Irelands too since, that have also passed away, so I must not entirely complain. But the world of my youth

142

is wiped away, as if it were only a stain on a more permanent fabric. I do not know where this Ireland is now. I hardly know where I am. My father's country had first a queen to rule it, and then a king, and then another king. It was a more scholarly, a more Shakespearean world, it was more like a story. Of course my father was part and parcel of that story, and no one wants to hear it now. People have other thoughts now. But they do not know all that they have lost. They tell the children in school how good the things of the present are, how much better than the terrible days when queens and kings of Great Britain and Ireland ruled us. They tell them about those fierce gunmen, Collins and De Valera, those savage killers in their day that thought nothing of murdering each other and far less of killing the likes of my father. Such days of absolute terror as we had in Dublin in those times, when the shadows of people shot at by soldiers of every hue, by snipers of every persuasion, as they wandered up the brown avenues and streets of our dark capital, would turn out in the light of morning to be mere drinking men wandering home, or worse, night-workers, women and young men, re-turning from their shifts in the cobbled glooms. Why, I myself and my sisters Maud and Dolly had to duck behind a quarter mile of sandbags along Dame Street to reach the gates of the Castle, with the young soldiers on sentry duty laughing at us, delighted by the spectacle no doubt now and then of our garters and stockings, and the unseen snipers firing betimes from their crow's-nests and niches in the old buildings of the city, firing at three young slips of girls. And because the young Tommies were sometimes handsome, we laughed too, and laughed at death, and scurried along, and laughed, and when we gained the castle yard we laughed loudest, and hugged each other, and we might be only returning haphazardly from a shopping expedition to buy bread and meat for our father's tea.

We had had a settled world enough, and we saw the Viceroy stream in through the gates in earlier times with all his bright and golden retinue, we watched our father drill his bright-booted men about the parade ground, recruits and shooflies and sergeants and inspectors and supers and chiefs like himself, and we saw the companies of the army wheel about, and make their music, and their shouts. And the milk dray came up through the frosted mists of every winter morning, and brought in the chill milk to the families that were ensconced in that castle, all those families, Irish and English, Scots and Welsh, and all their ceremonies and importances. It was a little watered and milky world in the middle of the distressed city, paupers and beggars everywhere, poverty everywhere, but also a strange gaiety, a strange peace, people of the beautiful Dublin sunlight, though it was rain mostly afflicted the roofs of that city. And that was the world that Willie died to protect, from the ambitions and ravages of the Kaiser, who was our king's cousin for all that. He died in mud like a beast for us, our Willie, so that everything could continue as before, and despite that he did that, and gave his life, it never did.

This is the world of thought I bring into Kiltegan village, hardly a metropolis to rival anywhere, though when my father was a child he said he thought it was as grand as Rome or Byzantium itself. We have passed the village gate of Humewood, which White Meg my grandfather used as entrance when he was steward there, because the steward's house is just yards there within. I think after all I did see him in my girlhood, though he died when the century was but five or six years old, so I might have been the little boy's age when I saw him. Oh, never a word did he speak as he came up the village road, so people say, like it was a song, nor looked right nor left, nor greeted nor offended anybody, but fetched himself in the gates of the estate as if a sort of solitary God. Because of course, thinking on the reason now, he was the link between the grand and polished owners of Humewood and all the plethora and generality of working people, the estate carpenters, the stonemasons, the coppicers like Sarah's own father, the tillers, the gravel men, the fencers, the roofers, and even the great host of gardeners that pulled the granite levellers across the acres of lawns, and tore out plants and planted in new ones in a dizzying cycle, though on some estates the garden workers were thought to be domestic and part of the household. Those house people my grandfather never approached, they were the hosts belonging to the head housekeeper and the head butler. Sixty servants roamed the great house in my grandfather's day, and nigh on two hundred men worked on the thousands of acres, and most had houses in the village or within the closely pointed walls. And those two hundred were the army of my grandfather.

All gone, all changed, all thrown away. Silence has generally fallen. Oh, on many an old topic. There is a solitary lady now living there, the last descendant of the original Humes, and she does not even bear the name. Who knows if she is lonely or content? She has a handful of servants now and there seem to be less of a force to go to harvest and go to sow, and yet she does well enough. The Land Commission and the new laws have surely trimmed her acres, but not as bad as other places. Seven generations of stewards were my people, and it is as if the story was never told, never heard, not even lingering enough to be forgotten, much less mourned.

This is why I am wary of bringing my thoughts into the village, though thoughts are silent. Because I suppose the general story of Kiltegan has knocked us off our perches, and there are people to enjoy that, and watch and wait for a chance word misplaced, mis-said.

To my eyes this is a ruined place. The walls still stand, but they are drear and painted only by the rain. The promised land is sore neglected.

The children have borrowed my silence as they do. The boy carries my purse at half mast, not exuberant now, casting an eye about at the seeming emptiness of the houses. The road is roughly tarred, and motor cars and trucks have torn at its edges, and the neat old cobbles of yore peep out like wide, blind eyes. You have to watch out for melted patches, or they will ruin your shoes.

Still and all, old thoughts aside, it is Kiltegan. The general shapes are true, and it is childhood also for me to walk here, despite everything, despite my bitter mind. I bought bull's-eyes here and Peggy's-legs also with my own father when he was yet a young man, visiting his home district in the summers with his single boy and three-fold belles of girls. The policeman, in his summer civvies, in times all fled.

Oh, what a mix of things the world is, what a flood of cream, turning and turning in the butter churn of things, but that never comes to butter.

The children race into the village shop, the bell ringing out with a metal sound across the once-metalled street. At least in here nothing has been changed. The jars of boiled sweets still hypnotize the children after school. Even the newcomers to the shelves, the factory bread in its grease-proof wrappings, seem old sights now. Who would have thought it, years ago, that a woman would not wish to bake her own bread, that source of pride and difference, like the very waters of your own well, sweeter and better than all other wells of the parishes. Sweeter and better was your own bread, and yet here they reside, these trim, similar, thin-crusted loaves that everyone wants to buy. Nevertheless, still on the counter sits the ribbon box, the very selfsame box that used to torment Dolly and Maud and me, our hands sweating at the thought of touching the blue, the red, the yellow ribbons. You would dream in the hot nights of that box and see in your dreams the many coloured bands spilling from the plain wood, spilling and whirling in your dreams. I hardly know why, now! A sprat of colour for a hat, a summer flourish. Oh, the ways and manners of our youth grow strange and small.

'Annie Dunne,' says Mrs Nicodemus.

'Ma'am,' I say. She is ever just Ma'am for some reason, perhaps for that her first name is Honoria, and her last that strange Greek name she got from her husband, as full a Wicklow man that ever was, but whose great-grandfather was a traveller in linens in Ireland that settled at length in Rathdangan.

Mrs Nicodemus is small and straight, and the curiosity is, she also like me has a slight bow in the back, but this is said to be caused by an injury as a baby, when she was dropped by her father when the midwife gave him a hold of the newborn child. Therefore she could not be said to be in a position to hand on her affliction and indeed her sons and daughters are perfect and true. Moreover she is so pretty, or was, that it makes her affliction like a graceful note, like the flaw in a beautiful woman's face, the beauty spot as it is called. Beautiful as she was, I know she does not like me, though I do not know the reason for it.

'This is the sort of weather now we live for in Ireland,' she says, in best shopkeeper fashion, No doubt she has said this or something like it a score of times this day. She says it with conviction, with the force of poetry, with a strange, muted passion, almost as if to drive me back with the truth of it, to banish me from her tidy and odorous shop. It smells of caraway and oatmeal, of nutmeg and cloves, strong, clingy smells indeed, and the softer smells of tea chests, of eggs in their trays without washing, straight from the warm places of the hens, such eggs as I have often brought down to her when my favourite hens have offered a surplus and a bounty, in particular, the best of the Rhode Island Reds, Red Dandy herself, a hen so productive now and then that I wonder she can still walk.

'Oh, yes,' I say, glad for the neutral haven of a topic like the weather — which is the purpose of such talk. I could not say, Honoria Nicodemus, I hate you for the luck of your bowed back, and your shapely children, and your husband's kisses, though this is what I think. So instead I will agree with her about the weather, which of course is remarkable. And then I remember hearing, from Sarah maybe it was, that Mrs Nicodemus just recently was given ill news from Doctor Byrne, who has found a lump as big as a turnip in the region of her stomach, which she will have to go to the hospital in Baltinglass to have examined. So now I am looking at her with slightly different eyes. I am thinking of the possible suffering of that news, and how bright and normal she is now with me and the children. Indeed she leans her little self on the old worn counter polished by all the hands and the generations of the hands of Kiltegan — even my childhood prints and

those of my sisters must be deeply there —
and smiles down her sunny face into the
children's faces, and all fear is banished
from them, especially the fearful little boy,
and she reaches without even looking for
readied-up bags of little sweets she has behind her, most likely for the schoolchildren
when they emerge at ten past three.

'There,' she says. 'What pretty smiles.
And these are Trevor's children? The boy
is the spit.'

'I am not,' he says. 'I wish I was. When I
grow taller than him he is going to send me
away.'

'Oh, never,' she says, 'that will never
happen. Never, ever,' she repeats, like an
article of belief, almost sadly, almost sadly.

'I will have to pack my bag then,' he says,
'though I have no bag yet.'

'Good boy,' she says, 'good boy. Time
enough for bags,' she says, 'isn't that right,
Annie? And my two eldest in Chicago now.
Think of that. Only yesterday they were
little lads like him, going about.'

And she shakes her head. Why does she
not like me, I wonder? What is it about me
that offends her, or troubles her even? I
wish I knew. I am thinking suddenly of my
brother Willie as she talks, the horrible
sadness that struck my father, that struck

me and my sisters when they sent back his uniform from France. They sent it back to us. It still had the marks of the mud on it, though there were also little slivers of something like mica in it. He had been killed, we thought, in a district like our own, where granite lies under the clays of the fields. The mica was scattered in the dried mud like silvers, like stopped snow. She will have waked her boys too, when they went to America, cried and cried for the loss of them in her bed, as if they had died.

There is more that should join us than keep us apart. But that can never be.

'Do you want anything more?' she says. Maybe she thinks it is frivolous and wasteful of my time to come all the way down to Kiltegan for bags of sweets. Maybe I do myself. But I cannot risk more than the three halfpence I pay her for the sweets. And why have I carried Billy Kerr's Peggy's-leg all the way also, as if it were a stick of explosives, as if it cannot be given to children? Again, again fear. Suddenly I am a puzzle to myself. I am frowning, I am sure, with perplexity. She is looking at me closely, quietly, as at a woman washed up on a little island of sudden ignorance.

'I, I . . .' I say, not very helpfully.

'I am going to go on with the sectioning of the tea, if you want nothing more?' She smiles now clearly. She is very pretty, even at her age. Fifty, fifty-five. Lucky, lucky, despite her flown sons. I see behind the counter she has been using a wooden ladle to fill pound bags of leaves from a great chest. Heavy tea is bad tea, they say. Because the damp will have got into it. A tea chest is lined with special paper, so the air goes out but no moisture in. Like a good house should be. The Indians, the Chinese, far away, growing tea for us here in Kiltegan. Crossing the impossible oceans. Clippers. My father knew all those things. He understood the origins of things. He used to say, we gave to the English cathedrals their roof beams. He said in the long ago, Merlin the magician stole the stones of Stonehenge from Kerry. And staves in their millions for barrels. Wood and stones to England, but they had given us the potato, in the person of Walter Raleigh. It was a fair exchange. The hatred between the islands had no sound base, he said. More to-ing and fro-ing than anyone knew, marrying, melding. We were the one people, secretly, he said. It was the fact of the secret that was killing the country, he said, in his later days. He was so full of sorrow. He was hurt in himself, wounded, deep, deep, down deep. For forty years he rose up through the ranks, keeping the peace, guarding, watching. Then everything he knew was burned and razed. It burned and razed the odd house of his mind. Never the same, never the same.

'Annie?'

I am startled now, by my own reverie, being woken from it. The two children are looking up at me, waiting for a sign.

'Oh, yes,' I say, 'no, we were, I was . . .' I don't know what I am saying. She smiles again and sinks back from the counter and takes up her ladle, and begins again her measuring. 'Willie, you see,' I say, '— I am sorry, sorry about your boys in Chicago, that's what I was thinking.'

'How do you mean?' she says, with a distinct, bladed tone in her voice.

'It was coming round in my head — I was thinking of it, how —'

'Are you mocking me, Annie Dunne?'

Of course I am appalled. Why am I trying to offer sympathy when the question is long settled no doubt in her mind? I must be mad, unhinged. What is wrong with me? Of course this is why she dislikes me. I have no grace, no truth, no womanly understanding. I am not a mother. I am a humpbacked woman that might make a humpbacked child. I am not like her, or any other human person. Moreover, I do not really feel sympathy for her, I feel it for myself. I am a charlatan, and in my emotions maybe almost a cretin. It is a terrible thing, to be there in her shop like a cretin. Will the Lord not save me?

'I am not mocking you, Ma'am. Please excuse me.'

I sound like a mere serving woman, a low sort. I herd the children out. The bell rackets merrily behind me. When I glance back through the fresh murk that the sunlight makes of the interior of her shop through the dusty window, I see immediately that she is not moving. The ladle does not glisten, it is made of wood, but something glistens there. Was there a brooch on her breast? Something is starry there, glistening, appearing and disappearing. I am a great fool. With my made-up sailor and my words in the wrong place and time.

'Thank you, Auntie Anne, for the beautiful sweets,' says the boy. 'Thank you, thank you.'

Soon we gain again the sanctuary, as you might say, of the green road. High up the heat runs along the rim of the woods, making the green colours fume up into the sky. The children have eaten their sweets. The new wrens, even tinier they seem than last year's, are bobbing about in the hedgerows like fat corks. Blue-tits, yellow-tits, and some brown bird I do not know the name of, try to blend themselves with the shades of the hawthorn and the scrubby ash trees. This is lower Kelsha. By rights we are citizens of Kelshabeg or Little Kelsha, under the bare wide coat of Keadeen. It is from Keadeen we used to gather the sprigs of purple heather in the old days, carrying them up to our rooms in Dublin Castle, sometimes having them sent up by the Wicklow bus, all as touch of home. The smell of the heather brought your Wicklow with you into the stony streets, the yellow and grey of Dublin town. As a child I used to think of it on the bus as if it were an animal itself in a paper bag. And I am sure the bus driver never thought twice about it. Such things do not seem daft to country people.

The bell flowers are just beginning to show their proper blooms at the tops, and the closed flowers in the middle of the stems are nearly right for bursting. I am showing the little boy how to do it, how to hold the bud softly and then suddenly close your fingers, making that satisfying noise. He cannot get the hang of it. He pesters me to keep showing him, but there begins to be only delay in the matter, and no pleasure. I try to coax them on. He gets more and more anxious and bothered. Now I am beginning to sweat under my dress, the heat is taking advantage of me, the road is lengthening against me as it rises into the trees. Once there were many cabins along here, Mary Callan's is almost the last of the proper one-roomed places. But when you go from a cabin of mud walls, the rain soon washes it away, till no trace is left. A one-roomed cabin abandoned, as the occupant heads off for America or the graveyard, or England, passes away from its corner of the land like a mere stain drying and crumbling. It was these people had the fiddle music and the fun, that played the road bowls in great crowds in the evenings, the younger boys massed on the banks of the road, cheering and shouting, longing to be old enough to play, and be the new hero. All that flock is gone. And in November, around the sixth, when the month of harvesting the spuds was over, there was that great week of visiting, when every group of cabins endured a fit of neighbourly hunger for each other's company, and Jack would go to Joe a couple of nights, and then Joe to Jack, and tremendous dancing there was, and we as girls though we were better people, hung at the poor half-doors in that democratic manner children have, and feasted our eyes on the jollity. And the odd night we would be gathered in among the fold of those labouring people, and stewardships and Dublin jobs would be forgotten, and me and Dolly and Maud and Willie, too, would swirl about on the rough flagstones of some provisional house, and dance, and feel the colours of the hewn rafters and the spidery thatch, the crust of whitewash on the stony walls, the streaming yellows and reds of the fire against the gable, feel those colours enter into our hearts and souls, and we would be made free as new wrens.

The little boy has stopped on the road behind us. He is weeping. When I go back to him I find he is weeping rather angry tears, if anything. The panic rises in me again. Is this the oranges, the true effect of the oranges? Am I about to find out something? I must be resolute, know my own mind, speak sensibly to them.

'What is it, childeen?' I say. 'What is it?'

He is staring down into the moss and water of the ditch.

'I've sent it down to Australia,' he says. 'Because you would not teach me the bell flowers.'

'What have you sent down to Australia?' I say.

'Oh, where is Auntie Anne's purse now?' says the little girl.

'Where is the purse?'

'You would not talk to me or listen, or stop again on the road. It has been sent away down to Australia.'

'Down in the water?' I say, astonished. I pull up the layers of my dress and cardigan and shove my right arm deep into the filthy ditch. A brown-black slime dresses the arm instead. I moil my fingers around among no doubt the tadpoles and the beetles and the leeches, until they close on the soggy leather of my purse. Out I haul it. It is ruined and unhappy-looking, like a frog killed by a heart attack.

'What do you mean, Australia?' I say, a surprising and suffocating anger rising in me.

'Isn't Australia upside down in the ditch?' he says, with a mollifying innocence.

But well-nigh savagely I turn from him.

Not a word will I speak, I tell myself, from this turn of the road to the pillars of our gates. I will not even look behind. They have both changed. It will never be the same again. The fairies have taken my little ones, these are only monsters, with their indifference to purses and their talk of oranges.

I march on, nursing my outrage. But, after all, he is only a mite. Who thinks that Australia is under the ditch! I expect if Australia really were under the ditch, I would have gone there years ago. And worn a hat with hanging corks against the flies. Beside the well-known wastes and billabongs.

I feel at sea and frightened again, but I cannot be their enemy, I cannot and must not. I am at the gates and all anger has gone. It is like dirty water flung out of a basin. I wish heartily I knew more about the world. I should maybe write to their mother and father. But how would I frame the words?

The little boy is staring up at me. I go back the few steps to him, to his long face. He is smiling, without mirth. He wants me to be smiling too, because my good graces are essential to him. I reach down and put my hand on the back of his head and pull

161

him gently to my apron.

'Child, child,' I say.

The little girl is stranded there on the road. The rush of summer weeds and grasses seems to blaze around her spindly legs. There is nothing to her. She is only a notion of humanity, a suggestion. Wicklow is wild with green and brown all about her, the colours fly up. The breeze tries softly to arrange her hair. I stand there holding the boy and looking at her, not knowing what to do.

'Australia!' he says, 'Australia!'

I laugh, no doubt like a sheepdog, like Shep himself, still collapsed in his sunspot on the yard. Oh, let us step through the ditch into Australia, and run with the kangaroos, and see the koalas, and cross the limitless emptiness of the interior. Let us go there, and dance with the convicts and be Australians, and meet again, I am sure, some of those fled denizens of the Kelsha cabins, that had the music and the dances in their keeping, and the great, lost happiness of that week in November when the spuds were safely saved.

Chapter Nine

No sign of Sarah in the house and yard, no sign of a killed chicken ready near the fire, to make our new stew. The fire itself has burned low, but that is my task and therefore my neglect. Carefully I build back the wall of turves, and roof it for good measure. Maybe the killed and plucked hen is under a dish on the dresser, but no. Something has made her, forced her, to abandon her task. Did the tinkers return? Most unlikely. The yard is strange and quiet, though I hear Billy snorting in his byre. The calves are bigger now and gone from the shed and will be frisky in the far garden, as we call it. The hens in general are pecking about between the pack-stones. They do not look like hens who have lost one of their number, and indeed when I count them, they have not. There is always a trace left among the hens when one has been murdered, I often think a resentful glare in those glassy eyes. Perish the day when we must consign the great Red Dandy to the pot. But the legs of hens get yellower, their lives are circumscribed like our own. I cast my gaze across the nearer fields, but no sign there of Sarah either. This is not a good feeling, the Sarahless farm.

It is a curious irritation to do another's share of work. But the gap in the tally of tasks must be filled, just as if it were a gaping hole in a field fence. The weight of the day, the collection of things and happenings that make a day, will not hold true with something left undone. It is a fact that you feel in your bones, in your water. It cannot be ignored.

Out into the peaceful yard I go, having sent the children before me to search the secret places of the hay barn, where the trap now looms alone, for whatever eggs may be hidden there. Hens take great pride in eggs. They covet them, though, like chicks. They do not always want you to find them. So you would think.

Perhaps their simple hearts tell them to find out-of-the-way corners and shelves and niches, against the predations of foxes and mice and rats. So the children must insert their warm arms into dark gaps, and feel about for the still-warm orbs secreted there, and triumphantly extract them. Perhaps we are like very comprehensive murderers to the hens, not only seeking the older ones for stews, but quenching all possibility of life from vulnerable eggs. Yet this thorough-minded enemy strides out in the evenings with the apronful of grain. We must puzzle them greatly.

Having spied an individual a little heavy with her years, one of the regular replacement birds we buy from time to time in Baltinglass fair, I corner her in the yard, where the walls of the calf shed and the hay barn make an angle. She seems to know well her fate. She skithers and dances, making a rush here and there which I block with counter-steps. We are dancing now in the yard, a funny dance of death.

Now I am within a farthing of her, and hold out my arms and gently but swiftly grasp her under the head.

I would not like to recount the look of pure horror that grips the hen, although in truth hens always bear a horrified expression, as if life in general was a thing of fear. She is living and breathing, she is growing old, the intervals between eggs is sadly widening, even the mighty cock himself must be growing weary of her, defeated by her gathering barrenness.

What would it be if some knowing farmer were to find out the barren women of Kelsha, and corner us in our yards, and wring our necks?

I lift her from the stable earth with caring quickness and shake her firmly, with a properly vicious, circular movement. The neck breaks immediately. She hangs from my efficient hand, her days of living done.

With a sigh, I must admit, I sit myself in the shade of the cow byre on a three-legged stool, and begin to pluck her.

It is then I see the little boy in the cowl of dark within the barn, watching me. His face shows nothing, one way or another. My right hand grips her now on the lower neck, the head hangs down, a droplet of crimson blood gathers on her loose red comb, my left hand by long familiarity flies from feathers and out, giving firm plucks, wrenching the quills from their tight roots. The pink skin, almost white, puckers up into a little mountain, then slowly falls back, smooth again but for the general wrinkles of a hen.

Nice and fat she is, with soft muscles. She is just right for boiling, and will make an excellent stew.

The little boy slowly approaches, leaving the summer darkness of the barn, his eyes fixed on the stripping hen. The white feathers fly about the yard, birdless and free. You could save those feathers and wash them well and use them to re-stuff a bolster, but I am not in thrifty mood. I pluck and pluck.

The little boy hangs a side of his rump on the chopping block, with its thousand stripes of the axe, and never offers a word, his face unchanging, like, it occurs to me, Matt when he is painting. I have watched Matt working the odd time secretly, noting how he does not move his face except to lick his lips, his left foot forward of his right as he stands at his easel in a summer meadow as may be, capturing some instance of beauty he has found in our Wicklow. I have watched him secretly from behind a tree, and loved something about him then, the peace and the power of him, the unsmiling happiness. It was thus that Maud encountered him those long years ago in St Stephen's Green in the heart of the city, ensnaring the duck pond onto his special watercolour paper as if he were alone in the heart of the mountains. I understand what took a hold of her. Even now when she is dead and he is surely sixty-six years of age, and all their kisses done, age falls away from him when he painting, time falls away, even I might hazard the very cut of his clothes, the present century, all that incidental matter. And Matt is there as the eternal creature, raptly working.

Something of this now stills the features of his grandson, watching my working hands as if he too were painting it, recording it not for himself necessarily, or for anyone, except perhaps the unknown memory of his God.

At dusk Sarah returns, I know not from whither, as the saying goes. The coming night is just pockets of hints in the sycamores. The fields about, the lower woods, are failing in my eyesight. Inside the kitchen the poor departed hen bubbles in the big pot. She has been dismembered and beheaded. Swedes and parsnips, potatoes and carrots, have joined her funeral. Dido herself, the queen of Carthage, burned on a pyre as Aeneas sails away, could not have felt more honoured.

I have given her spuds without black eyes and the smaller, sweeter carrots. The three of us, small boy and girl, myself the general, have bestowed on her the stew of stews.

They have found all of thirteen eggs, a magnificent haul, ranged now on the dresser for Sarah's return, the children say. They sense the unusual absence and naturally as children they assume some strange sadness in the grown-up, which the harvested eggs will banish.

She comes in through the gloom of the door, it must be well past eight. It is not true dusk, the proper dusk of night, but the artificial dusk this farm endures when the sun goes over beyond our mountain, and all the sloping field and trim of woods is thrown into shadow. It is as good as dusk, though sunlight remains on further farms, looking bright and covetable on the plain, brighter farms than ours, the faraway fields no doubt of the proverb. Well, faraway fields indeed are greener than the fields of Kelshabeg, in the summer evenings.

'Sarah,' I say.

What else can I offer? I do not wish to scare her, blame her, offend her. I must be neutral like those foreign diplomats that sometimes visited the Castle, dignitaries that would neither praise not criticize, for fear of war — or so my father would say. One misplaced word might plunge all Europe into chaos, he said, and that was the sorry life of a diplomat. We used to watch them from our windows with great anticipation, hoping for visible disaster. But they did not look sorry to us, with their cheerful faces, and their huge official vehicles. Often in those years countries came and went, as did our own, names and borders changing, but it did not affect the cheerfulness of diplomats, as far as we could judge.

She passes through the kitchen without speaking, sadly not registering the haul of eggs, and on through the door into our bedroom, and closes the thin door quietly.

I have sprinkled water on the flagstones and brushed them, yard by yard, as is my custom. There is a manner to sweep a floor. My mother's grandmother's floor was clay, red clay, and that took expert sweeping, but if done well it is as clean as stones. I have tidied away the few stray objects of the day, the Bible that Sarah must have been perusing, a tin box with nothing in it. I have the wooden box of socks for darning by my legs, and am sitting fairly hunched by the lowering fire. The big darning needle passes with a satisfying ravishment through the thick, still heel of one of Sarah's working socks, that lines her boots. She has not emerged, but is lying, I have no doubt, on our bed, immobile, quiet, staring at the old egg-blue ceiling boards. It would not be the first time for such strangeness, and I must allow it. If not for me, sometimes I think the country home at Baltinglass would beckon for her.

I feel some accomplishment in the fact,

though it bears to me the shadows of my father's last days with me in Lathaleer, before his final outbreak and decline. It seems I must be sometimes daughter and cousin to the mad, or nearly mad. But I blame neither that old policeman nor my cousin Sarah, it is the declensions of age that are at fault, the very faulty arrangements of our Lord for such as we become. If this is blasphemy then the Lord will have to forgive me.

My father in the old kitchen at Lathaleer raved and waved his ceremonial sword, with his shirt rended by himself and his trews bestained by urine, and cursed himself and my own life. I thought he would kill me, and when he reached the height of his raving he begged me to kill him, with the sword, across his poor addled head like a sword of Damocles. I could not do that, but some would say I brought a worse judgement on his wits, by putting him to the county home in Baltinglass, with the help of Matt. And there in darkness of mind and pitiful reduction, he died. He that once kept all of B division in Dublin, with responsibility for the castle herself, as he would say, all quiet and shipshape for viceroy and king. I would not willingly put Sarah to such sorrows, and if I can stand between her and whatever ails her mind, just now and then, I will have paid her better for the niche she has given me, than any thousand eggs from a Rhode Island Red.

The fire is sweet and red, like habitual garnets, or rubies strewn under black stones.

The little boy comes from the blackness of his room, slips in near beside me on Sarah's chair. I do not even look at him. He is like a mouse, a field creature I must not disturb. How small and trim he is, how neat his bending back. His legs hang from the seat of the chair.

'Auntie Anne,' he says. 'I am sorry for the purse. I am sorry.'

'Why did you throw it in the ditch?' I say, at ease.

'Oh,' he said, 'the notion came into my head, and I just did it, like boys do.'

'I know,' I say, 'I know. Well, I did a worse thing, I must confess. And don't you tell your sister, I think she would not understand. You will understand, I am sure.'

'But what did you do?' he says, with fierce interest. The crimes of a grown-up!

'I stood at the margin of the scrubby wood, on the road there below, and I threw a Peggy's-leg that Billy Kerr gave me for you, I threw it as hard as I could, way, way into the tangle of the brambles and trees.'

'Why, Auntie Anne?' he says, fascinated.

'I don't know why. I just did it. Do you understand?'

'I do,' he says. 'I do.'

We sit there silently. The barn owl in the pines above us slowly sounds, feels his way through the darkness to us with his voice. That must be a lonely life. Other more human sounds are only the clumsy wind. The clock ticks on the dresser, the mice run about in the roof. A segment of turf puffs down into destruction. In all the houses of Kelsha will be sleeping forms, I am thinking of that: Mary Callan in what I imagine is her filthy bed, the old rabbit man above near the owl with his sad memories, all the kith and kin strewn along the green road in the stone houses, breathing and dreaming on their feather pillows. It is on the tip of my tongue to ask him about the oranges, him kneeling there between his sister's legs. But a voice in my head says, do not, do not.

'I suppose it is a crime to throw away another person's Peggy's-leg, Auntie Anne,' he says, without accusation.

'Oh, a crime indeed — a small crime. There are crimes and crimes. One time . . .'

'Oh, yes, Auntie Anne?' he says brightly, sensing a story.

'Well, one time, we had a dog. No, I should say, because it was in my father's time, when he was only a little boy like you, *they* had a dog. This dog was also called Shep. Anyway, this Shep killed a sheep, which was a very serious matter. It was my father found the dead ewe on one of the higher fields, just over the road from this farm, and he went back down and told his father, and his father said, "Go back up and put a rope around that dog's neck, and bring him down, Tom," — for that was my father's name — "and I will shoot him." Well, my poor father, just a mite of five, went back up the fields with a heavy heart, and put a rope around Shep's neck, ready to obey his father's wishes. But he had a great liking for that dog, and turned his footsteps up into the woods, and passed on in, just up here behind us, and disappeared.'

'These very woods? Oh, Auntie Anne. What happened?'

'Well, some hours passed and my grandfather began to be anxious. He was the steward there on the Humewood estate and he was a blunt, old-fashioned man, and many a time he had beaten my father.

He beat him one time with a cooper's band, a hoop of metal off of a barrel, and my father carried the scars of that beating on his back all his life.'

'My father never has beaten me,' says the boy. 'My father will not even kill a bluebottle, though bluebottles eat poos,' he says, gravely.

'These were other days. And my father would tell this story without rancour. When it began to grow dark that day and it was clear that the little boy was missing, my grandfather raised the district, and bands of people, cousins and neighbours alike, lit bright torches and scoured the fields about and called out my father's name — Tom! Tom! But there was never an answer. The night was pitch and cold, and my grandfather fell into a fever of disquiet, and he cursed himself for sending the lad on such a task. For even a rough man like the old steward had in him a tenderness that could be awoken by an emergency. He sent the men and women of the district out hither and thither with the torches, urging them on all the while, but alas, to no avail.'

'He was killed, he was killed!'

'No, child, he was not killed.'

The fire sputters and quarrels minutely

with itself on the hearth. Little visitors of flames run across the failing heaps.

'Well, well?' says the boy, eager to hear the fate of that other boy, in the long ago.

'My father himself had only a dim recollection of that night, but he did remember standing with the dog in a moonlit glade, standing all night with the dog, never moving, hearing, he said, in the distance now and then people calling his name. But he could not move or answer. What kept him standing there he could never say, but stand he did. The dog itself shivered in the cold, but he himself, my father, felt quite warm, quite strange, quite resolute, as if an enchantment had fallen on him, by the force of his affection for that dog.

'Near daybreak, at last, my father moved his legs. Down from the deep, dark woods he came, and out onto the sloping field. All about him the neighbours gathered, with their torches, saying his name, and calling out to the others below that he was found. But my father paid them no heed. He had it in his head that he would be shot too, now, along with the dog, for his misdeed, for the crime of his disobedience. And he was quite resigned to that.

'He came down the fields of Humewood towards his father's lodge. His father

176

emerged from the house below. How big and dark he looked! My father's heart shrank in his breast. The dog itself was whining on the rope, being dragged along, knowing well, you need not doubt, its own dark crime of killing the ewe.'

'And were they shot, the both?'

'When my father reached his father, one of those great hands went up, as if indeed to strike down the little boy, but no, it was to pull my father's head to him, and grip it with that fierce tenderness, and he lifted his own head and thanked his God for the deliverance of his son.'

Then the boy says an unexpected thing. It is only one stray word, but it comes forth as natural as a bubble in the well, up from the frothy mud. There is no sentiment in the word, he says it as plainly as he says anything. But it surprises me. It makes me wonder about him, if he hasn't something unusual within, some quaint understanding beyond his years, or despite them. He is what they used to call *seanaimseartha*, an old-fashioned child.

'Love,' he says.

Now I realize he has said it with a stain of desperation. I am disquieted again. The oranges, the oranges . . . The little boy sits by the moulder of the turf. He seems to be thinking, thinking on my words. I can almost hear his mind whirring, turning everything about, examining everything, deciding. His small hands grip the wooden edge. He is as still as a stone, overwhelmed, transfixed. Myself, I have not thought of that story for twenty years or more. Forty years maybe. It is strange how vivid it is in my mind. I can see the torches as I speak of them, see my grandfather in the door of the steward's lodge. Yet I was not there, I was not born, my father was only five years old.

'And what happened to the dog, Auntie?' he says.

'I do not know,' I say. 'My father never said. Or did he say my grandfather let it live, and never mentioned its crime again? There are crimes and crimes, you see, like I said. The story seems to stop at that door, father and son in their moment of . . .'

There is another spate of silence.

'Love,' says the little boy finally. He looks up at me now. There is a kind of pleading in his face. 'My father,' he says, like a brief, fragmented song he sings alone to himself, and is singing now for me, 'loves me.'

'Of course he does.'

'And he loves my sister.'

'Of course.'

'And he loves my mother.'

'He does, of course!'

'He does,' says the boy, with great satisfaction.

'Maybe you should wander into your bed now,' I say.

'All right,' he says, but doesn't move an inch.

So we sit there, listening to the owl. It must be in the mossy woods, but near, at the very margin of the trees.

'If you showed me the spot,' he says at last, the words heavy from being first thought, 'I might climb in after it.'

'After what?' I say.

'The lovely Peggy's-leg.'

'You would never find it.'

'That is sad, then,' he says without sadness.

'It is,' I say.

The little boy gets up and hugs me. He puts his short arms about me and hugs my bones. I stroke the black hair of his head, thinking of all past times, and present times, the river of time upon which we are merely carried, small boys and girls, loves expressed but rarely, loves confounded in the main.

Warm he is, warm, warm.

Perfect time, perfect time, perfect time, says the clock.

* * *

When he is gone, I sit there alone. 'My father loves me.' He loves his father, more than life, I am thinking. It is right and meet that a child should love his father so. A litany of love, but something is bothering, bothering me.

It is another story entirely, also a true one. When my father was a sergeant in the police force, he succeeded in arresting a man who had assaulted a little girl on Kingstown Pier. For this he was awarded two shillings by his superintendent. He had other money awards in his day, one of them for helping in the rescue of sailors off a stricken ship in Dublin Bay. That was easy to explain to us, three girls. But the other award was not so straightforward. Maud, being the eldest, was told the full story, and she, being our loyal sister, gave us all the details later in our beds. We were gripped and horrified. Assaulted, the very word — suggesting a sort of leaping. I could see that wolfish man in my mind's eye, vaulting through the air with bared teeth.

I know the little girl has not been assaulted in that sense by her brother. Her brother is only small. She was instructing him in the game, if anything. But if it is a

180

secret game, as it seemed, how did they come to begin to play it?

I go into my bed, and Sarah is awake and clear. She smiles her smile of a lost child.

'I was lying here thinking what was the worst thing ever befell me,' she says. 'And I cannot think what it was, unless it was the death of my mother.'

'God rest her,' I say, as decent people do.

'God rest her indeed,' says Sarah. 'But what was the worst thing ever befell you, Annie?'

'Oh,' I say, 'there has been a number of such things. The death of Willie, my father's troubles late in life, and then the death of Beatrice, Maud's daughter.'

'The death of Beatrice, Maud's daughter,' she repeats. 'And Matt's daughter.'

'And Matt's daughter too, of course. It was terrible for him, I know. But I think it was worst for Trevor. It was worst for Trevor, bring only small himself, and her brother.'

'It was worst for him,' she says, with the familiar tune of a topic discussed before, 'in that he was so small himself, and was blamed.'

'Yes, Maud blamed him. That was not right. He was only six. She was a baby. It's true he gave her the Scarlet Fever, but only out of love. A little boy does not understand quarantine. Didn't he feel just wonderful, and missing his sister. He was told, he was told not to go to her, with the infection still in him. But in he crept and kissed her, all in secret. And then when she died, he confessed what he had done, and Maud, Maud blamed him.'

'You were up there helping, weren't you, Annie, and you saw everything?'

'I saw everything, and felt everything. And I don't think little Trevor was ever the same idle, happy boy again.'

'No, but he is a fine man now.'

'A very fine. What has set you, Sarah, to asking these old questions?'

She sighs, deep and sad. I do not think that this is the daftness in her after all. She is very serious and still. Her old body is thin and warm beside me. I can feel the rough cotton of her nightclothes just against my right knuckles. I frown in the darkness, though there is moon and light as well tonight. That old unease creeps back. I sense also her trouble and pain, but on what head I do not know.

'Oh, I have been shaken by these recent days,' she says. 'I have tried to say otherwise, to you and to myself, but Billy throwing you out on the road, the tinkers and their menacing . . . Women alone, I am afraid, Annie.'

'Don't be afraid, Sarah.'

'I am afraid, and I am afraid.'

'Don't be.'

'I am, though. Women alone. It would be better if . . . if there was . . .'

'A man here? But there is no man.'

'No, there is none now. There were men here once. That carved out the fields and made the yard and put everything in place. They made the ship that we only sail. We are like the last sailors aboard, though. I am afraid. And I think I am right to be afraid.'

'Well, try and sleep now, Sarah. We must be churning in the morning, and scouring. A few dreams, Sarah, and when it is daylight again, your fear will be gone.'

'Maybe so, Annie.'

She is quiet now. I am quiet. My knees are jumping with painful energy, my back is reeking with soreness, rawness. It is strange. I am like the spring of the clock wound too far, all tight and stopped.

'Are you sleeping, Annie?' she says from under the blanket.

'I am not. I am worrying now.'

'Don't be worrying.'

'I am worrying about the girl. I wanted to ask you about the girl.'

'The girl,' she says. Then silence under the blanket. At length I imagine she must be asleep. But the old voice stirs out again.

'I am afraid,' she says, 'she is wounded. There is a wound in her nothing can heal. All you can do is watch over her. She needs watching over.'

'What do you mean, Sarah?' Because Sarah is wise in certain matters. She knows old medicines. She knows unguents. There was a time when she was valued for it, as an alternative to any doctor. But those days are gone. I had almost forgotten it was ever so. But her voice carries that old authority, and doubly frightening for that.

'What do you mean, Sarah?'

But this time the dog of sleep has fetched her. She is gone. I am left alone to think my thoughts, to wonder and wonder about the oranges.

It is a morning again of sun, heavy on the hands of the byre, the barn, the house. The red geraniums are slowly ekeing out their tight blooms. They begin to catch fire along the granite windowsills each side of the door. The whitewashed window-reveals and walls also excite their colour. It is a lovely thing, a favourite thing, although also you would think of the passion of Christ, of holy blood lying around an exhausted forehead on the cross, such are those drops of flowers.

From red geraniums to yellow butter I go.

I have boiled a pot of water on the kitchen fire and carried it into the dairy and now I fetch the big enamel basin and brush. In the little dairy as clean as a prayer, with its limed upper walls and wooden counter, I wield the scrubbing brush, mashing the stiff hair into the hard counter so that every hint of dust and grease is gone.

Down on my bony knees I do likewise for the flags, till the steam rises everywhere, and the room looks like a little chance wave has broken into it, and scoured it out, terrorized it with cleanliness. Since six o'clock Sarah has been churning, turning and turning the metal handle, listening to the slosh of the cream inside, over and over, till the sweat sits along her arms and on her big, bare face. She does not speak all morning and I am not inclined to wrench words from her. She never believes in that butter, and is convinced that only I have the knack of what she calls happy butter.

At last she gets the signal, a heavying up inside the barrel, a protest almost from the cream, as it gives up the ghost and becomes the different nature of the butter, only the whey washing about like a memory of cream. It is a delicious victory for Sarah. She gazes about with sumptuous pride, her own worst opinion disproved. This has happened a hundred times, and tomorrow she will be back to saying she has no knack for the butter, but no matter.

And that is a great moment, a moment of strange stiffness after long labour, and a releasing moment, and it is how I am sure the butterfly feels when at last it breaks from the discarded caterpillar, drying its wings and easily flying to become that graceful thing. And there is a grace in butter, how can I explain it — it is the colour we all worship, a simple, yellow gold.

And it is my job now to make the ingots of it, Sarah sort of fussing and hissing at the door, like an enormous goose. I roughly knock it into shapes like small turves, never touching with my hands, using the big wooden butter blade, and then the two little paddles as neat as oars, pushing and slapping and coaxing, till I have five good half-pounds, which I wrap in butter paper, and pop in the drip press to keep as cold as summer will let me.

In the old days we would take not only a sprig of heather from the hills back to Dublin Castle, to keep home near, but also a length of butter in a turn of paper. And in the butter was put the thorn from a blackthorn tree, to keep it from going off. You had to be mighty careful, when you got home to those echoing walls and court-yards, to fish out that sharp, devious little thing, before you put anything in your mouth.

And although Sarah is gripped in her si-lence, we are like two dancers, two doors opening and closing on perfect hinges, two creatures oiled in their actions, concerted, with one purpose, wonderfully adept, and in my case wonderfully happy. When you find me in the dairy, an old rook of a woman in a blue and white apron, the room immaculate, the sun excluded but honouring the gap of the door with rinsing light, you will find only the picture of hap-piness.

And all the while there is that clean, clear smell, that remembers everything in the making of the butter — the meadow, the mouths of the milch cows, their secret stomachs, the grasses wrenched from their green selves, the milk in the soft warm udders, the odour of inside skin — all perfect and mixing together into one laden smell, a smell that in its nature is the very opposite of mould and rot, that makes the dairy ring like a guitar.

'Annie, dear,' says Sarah at last.

'Yes, dear?' I say. She stands in the sparkling door, the light showing through her summer dress. She has been wearing that dress, washing and repairing it, for thirty years. Her summer dress, with the faint blue pattern of roses and lines, growing ever fainter. One day it may be a plain white dress.

'I have been talking to Billy,' she says.

It is as if I have already heard her speech. Maybe I have rehearsed it in my dreams unbeknownst. Still and all I can't believe it, I do not wish to believe it, and at heart I don't believe it.

'I have been talking to Billy, and we have said . . . things, to each other, and it may be that we will reach an understanding.'

'The worst thing that ever befell me? Is this why you were talking on that topic last night? To see if what you were going to say might . . . might, kill me?'

'Kill you?'

'I am only a light — I am . . . How light is a feather, Sarah? One of those slight little feathers from under the hen's belly, that she leaves often on her eggs, a sort of tiny flag . . .'

But I have lost her — I have lost myself. I am trying to tell her, what? That time has thrown me from my own family, that Matt has thrown me from my former niche, that Kelsha is my last refuge, my last stand, that the half of her warm bed is all my desire, that I will be glad to go to my grave from this small yard, carried out between the pillars with their nesting stones . . . That always I have expected to be cast off, discarded, removed . . . My hurts and thoughts discounted. That we have, she and I, not a marriage of bodies but a marriage of simple souls, two women willing to do the work of a hard subsistence farm, to dig out the potato ground, to milk the milch cows, to tend the fire, to fetch the water, even when she is dark and dour to take her tasks to myself, and recognizing that there is no honey of man here, no strong, hard limbs of man to crush us underneath him, and give that crazy pleasure that we have only heard tell of, that holy ecstasy that was not accorded to us, recognizing the losses and lacks, that we have a

189

world here, a way, an admirable life enough . . . But, none of these things I utter. None. Because I cannot get the words out, and if I could, she would not hear them as I intend them. It would be like Mrs Nicodemus, with other meanings than I intend.

So the only way to answer now will be by deviousness and counter-play. The only way to answer will be to confound this Billy Kerr in his evil plans by actions more dark and dexterous than his own. Poor, slight, long Sarah. Does she think it is for her he has walked this strange walk?

She is standing there, lost herself, open-mouthed, afflicted. How ridiculous she seems. Sixty-one, reeled in by forty-five. He must have some stomach now, that same Billy Kerr, to think for the sake of a little farm that he can lie in the nights beside this old woman with her long, clean bones like the pillars of the courthouse in Baltinglass. That he can set his mouth on hers and whisper to her in the dark. I am almost laughing. Then the bad words rise up, surprising even me.

'Sarah Cullen, do you think he wants you, an old woman without a hint of youth, or this farm of thirteen acres?'

'What, Annie?'

'What has he been saying to you, Sarah, that makes you think you can do this thing? Are you going to walk down to Kiltegan church and stand in a white dress before poor Father Murphy, and ask that old, benighted priest to wed you to this man? This man who is only a scoundrel in a pair of farm boots, the do-everything, the lackey of my cousins, the Dunnes of Feddin. What will all the people of the district say? Don't you think they will laugh at you, be disgusted by you, their stomachs turning at the thought of you, Sarah Cullen, marrying such a man?'

'Why, Annie? Cannot any person marry? Is it a crime? Annie, Annie, is it a crime — I did not know?'

Her words are so simple, small, and low. Whispery. I feel myself the greater criminal by far than Billy Kerr. I should have kept my own opinions to myself, and let this story take its course, as I have always allowed every story that has come to me. She is open and raw to my wounds. That is why I have wounded her. Because I am so well able. These are the actions of a wicked mind. And as suddenly I am assailed by other fears, the plain fact we have these two children in our care. Am I going to be thrown off before their father returns for them? Will there be a need now for letter-writing and telegrams, and letting down of people, and all the rest? And what will befall me then? Who will take me? Will heart and body fail, and the county home open its doors for me, like my poor, discarded father in his day? That evil action answered by this, that by throwing him away I am to be thrown away in turn, unloved, unwanted, and unseen.

Chapter Ten

But maybe there is something that can be done, gently and truly, to unlock this dam of branches and rubbish in the river of Sarah's simple life. After all, I am her guardian, plain and simple. She took me in not only because I had no pillow upon which to lay my thinning head, but because no doubt she felt the threat in the countryside around her, the threat even of the dark and wind, of the day when she might wake and feel the strength not as much at her beck as heretofore. Oh, she is a mighty girl, strong and unchanging and true, but even an old wall of massive stones will start to lose its power when the old lime washes from between the gaps and the clever rain goes in and makes its secret mischief. Then one morning you go out to find a corner of your barn asunder, and great stones twisted and cracked from their ancient beds, and the work of dead hands undone.

An unexpected calm takes a hold of me. This daft marriage is too odd, too disquieting. The whole of Kelsha, Kiltegan and Feddin would be made uneasy by it. There wouldn't have been the like in these parishes in all the decades of existence. It is something you might hear about in Dublin — not even Dublin, which in many ways is only another country town, being stuffed with indigent country people, but all those places that are made clear in the odd risky book I might have come across. Maud used to keep them in her knicker drawer, one by one from the library in Donnybrook, and even unknown to her I would filch them out now and then and have a quick peruse. And when the pictures came first to Dublin, there were mighty terrible films to see, of wild divorcees and the like, and extravagant goings-on in far-flung places like California, where all the houses seemed to be made with strict right angles and all their furniture was smooth and shining. That is something you notice when you are reared in Ireland. I often, too, in the afternoons took the tram into O'Connell Street and went into the Savoy, and sat alone in the great terraces of seats and watched an almost incomprehensible picture, in the company of a hundred other women like me, and on Wednesdays all the cooks and parlour maids would be there, on their day off, dressed to the nines, but not quite ever the nines of the women on the screen. And in those stories strange things happened, and you witnessed strange things, and one of the things you would love most was when Gary Cooper kissed a girl, Gary Cooper that was like a stone himself, but who could melt a woman like lead in the roof of a burning mansion.

I am taking now all this experience of life and there is something in Sarah's declaration that makes me strongly suspect she could not have the support of anyone in her predicament. At the same time I feel a creeping guilt, and oddly enough the situation arouses in me a profound love for her, a reaffirmation of the respect and care I have for her, this side idolatry, as Ben Jonson says of William Shakespeare, according to my father. It is not only the memory I have of her as a girl, all clean and fresh as wheat with the moist seed still in it, as subtle as a bud, as clear as a sun shower, but the woman she is now, that I lie beside through all the seasons, and know so well, or think I do. And I know what is the matter with her, because it is the matter with me, that awful fear I feel she feels too, that fear heaped up around our hearts by so many things — age and our vulnerable sex and all the rest.

At any rate we are invited down to the Dunnes of Feddin for the tea-time and I will be able without announcement, without suddenly turning up in a state of anguish or any other undesirable state, to talk quietly to Winnie about it, Winnie who is the scholar and so wise, and after all, Billy Kerr takes her wages and is in her keeping, and even a wild dog like him has to obey the keeper of his bones.

At the same time I would be wise not to say anything first to Lizzie, who is the sister almost as strong as a man, and with the manners of a man, and who has used her fists on more than one occasion, once knocking a fencer to the ground at the back of their farm, because he was laying in the posts at too great distances in a spot he thought no one would notice. But of course that is how cattle get out, and she knocked him down in justice, and he accepted that.

Whereas May is too soft and nice, like her name, all white and frothy, silent and hard-working, all smiles and no words at all, though she tries hard to gabble responses to greetings, to remarks on the weather and the like, and really lives in the loving shelter of her sisters.

It is Winnie, both strong and gentle, with

all the characteristics of her sisters, and yet with the added virtue of wisdom, that may help me. After all she teaches their lessons to the children of Kiltegan, and not low and high babies, but the bigger ones who will go out to work when she is finished with them, so she is teaching tricky stuff, the very stuff you forget the moment you leave school, but no matter, like compound fractions and long division, long division which I could do at school but could not put myself to now, God forgive me.

The other thing that strongly settles me on this occasion is the boy and the girl. It is not just myself I have to fight for, as in the past, and always battles that I lost, but I must preserve where they are now, until their father comes for them. He has promised to return before the harvest, at the close of summer, when we will begin to be deepest at our labours, but who knows what struggles they may be enduring, what difficulties and what trials in the mazy city of London? Dublin to me holds no fears or mysteries, being virtually a Dublin woman in part myself, but I would not like to go down to the pier at Dunleary and take that big mail packet to England, I would not.

The children's grandfather, Jack O'Hara, travelled the entirety of the earth in the merchant navy, he has told me — grandfather on their mother's side — but we have always been stickers to home and loath to roam, always excepting the wild courage of my sister Dolly, who went to Ohio almost as an indentured slave, let us say a house servant on contract, and nearly broke my father's heart, or in fact did break it. Dolly, who was only five foot high, and prettier than many a lacquered film star, set off alone from the regretful arms of the Liffey, past the solemn figure of the Dowager Lighthouse, and the portly one of the Poolbeg, way beyond the furtive dog, crouching down ready to spring and savage you, that is the hill of Howth, and down to Cobh and out beyond everything she knew, to strange America. Because, she said, she could not bear the changes that befell us, the loss of my father's mighty job, the country that we knew, and at last, his very wits.

Dolly, Dolly, Dolly, in Ohio, my father cried.

So I keep the peace with Sarah in shipshape fashion. It is washday, so we spend the hours boiling sheets and blouses, and scrubbing at our and the children's garments in the zinc tub, and lathering and rinsing. For this we use almost the full measure of the rainwater in the barrel, because you would be killed going down to the well.

On washday the water bucket becomes as useful as a thimble, the deluge of water that is required.

At least in summer there is no rain paradoxically to ruin your efforts, at least not today, though every night this week the rain has fallen, as if in a furious frenzy to wash the earth. But there is good solid drying time in the daytime hours, and we spread our sheets with their gift of starch on the drying-bushes with confidence.

Sarah will gather them in in the late evening before the sun is gone, and tonight she will stand in the kitchen with the irons heating on their spotless grille by the fire, and iron the sheets till the starch in them dries and fixes them into objects like the thinnest metal, which is how we love our sheets. So that when you set a child under them, and tuck them in, they are gripped by those sheets as if in a strange embrace, and barely stir the whole night.

We speak but little all day, but there is nothing unusual in that. When the work is there, especially washday, which will go from six o'clock till late that night, words become unnecessary. We know the pleasant drills. When the sheets are dry you will see us other days in the yard or kitchen, holding our corners, and stepping to each other and stepping away in that old dance of folding, wordless, exact. Those dances are known now inside the bones.

Nevertheless I feel her pain and confusion, and certainly feel my own. We send the children to roll in the grassy sloping field, and when they are done with that we find other adventures for them, to keep them out of our hair. We stop only for cups of tea, slices of buttered bread and blackberry jam. When we are ruined by thirst, we throw down big mugs of our milch cow's milk. It is all in the day, it is nothing to us, except this new nag of hurt between us. Illusion or not, I sense my power over the situation, and flatter myself that she does too. I begin to feel so confident and strong, I think I would strike Billy Kerr with a bar if he strode in, and cleave him like a pig, and hang him in the byre from the pig hook, and bleed him, and shave his bristles for him, and make black pudding from his dark blood and all the rest of those ceremonies reserved for the killing of the munificent pig.

Leaving the wide white linen sheets

drying on the shocked bushes, we set off, the children and me, for my cousins' farm. I have at least discharged my share of the work, a heavy day of work it is, the washing. I have not abandoned Sarah just for argument, but stayed true to what is daily required of us. I am almost washed myself, to the inner bone, by the great effort of washing our world clean. And carry that righteous feeling to the lower road, the lower world.

A trim road of pines leads to their gate, an old iron affair with designs on it where the latch is. But the gate is locked and we must cross the mossy style, which delights the boy. Their farmhouse stands beyond, a square house in the centre of a muddy field. It is only the hooves of the cattle does that, because their yard teems with bullocks. They are always meaning to fence or ditch around their house, but the old garden has long since been wiped away by those hooves. Billy Kerr should be more bothered by that than he is, but then what is the measure of Billy Kerr? Once there were roses there, and lilies in the summer, orange ones, and fuchsia in droves, but no more. They are not seemingly those sorts of women that need a garden. I suppose they are strange women enough.

When their father died they stripped out the house of everything that spoke of him. But never said the why of it. Seemingly, they loved him while he lived. True, he kept all courting men away, till sense might say it was too late. He died of an apoplexy all the same, raging at some matter or other. He was buried beside his wife, forty years gone before him. Carpets and curtains went, to the bare wood. Maybe they meant to decorate again, and it has to be said that it was always a better house than Lathaleer, certainly than Kelsha, which is only a cottage. Feddin is a two-storeyed farmhouse with a little neat door. But they never did put new carpets and curtains in, and so their house now is like a great series of wooden drums — everything scrubbed clean, it must be said, they never tire of the scrubbing, but echoing and banging and rattling.

'Ah, Annie, dear,' says Winnie as we come into the wooden hall. She stands back then with a flourish and puts her two hands on her hips and gazes down on the children like they were miracles come into her abode. 'Lovely, lovely creatures,' she says.

'Indeed and they are, Winnie,' I say, laughing.

'Oh, they are, they are. They are . . . beauteous.'

Now, you can see her learning in a word like that. Her and my father had the same vocabulary, as I suppose myself and my father had too. Winnie and I like each other. We know what Hamlet is, we know who Bottom was, and like to laugh about it. True, I never read those books, but lapped such knowledge from my father's garrulous knees!

'Come in, come in, the whole crowd of you,' she says, like we were teems of people, 'come in.'

And she leads us into their bare parlour, with its old scratched windows and the window seats unflattered by cushions. The room cries out for care and embellishment, yet all the same I love their parlour. The very wood is so scrubbed and white, it is pleasing. And today, much to my astonishment, they have spread a starched cloth on their habitually raw table, an honour that would be difficult to explain to children, but I feel it, in fact I am wondering if they haven't been into Baltinglass to purchase it. And there are oddments of cups, blue and white and it must be confessed more cracked than not, and plates, and rough tea cakes and a big hot-looking kettle of tea. I can see the little boy is quite taken aback. To add to the deluge of new things, the rook-like shapes of Lizzie and May stand incongruously in each window frame, like vigorous statues. The light beams in from the clamour of sun outside, till their dresses look enormous and bizarre. The little boy almost cowers back. He lifts his small hands to defend himself against these visions, visions that melt down into mere old women when they step forward to try and kiss these rare sorts of visitor. Oh, I see that hunger in their eyes, the very hunger that has been satiated in me by having the boy and girl for these weeks, and if it has been hard work it is the look of sheer desire and wonderment and delight in my cousins that reminds me of my great privilege and access to joy. And suddenly, looking at these wildish women, with their startling hair and rough clothes, the backs of Lizzie's hands torn into scabs and wounds by maybe barbed wire, by God knows what manly labour, I am already thrown forward in spirit to late summer, when as sure as salt their father will come for them, and I will be a childless crone, a withered woman, all unmothered yet again.

'Good Lord above,' says the little boy, in

words I never heard from him before. 'How did you get those wounds?'

'It's only slits,' says Lizzie, 'it's only slits I got off of the plough!'

Then she bends as by right to get a kiss from this terrified child. Oh, such terror I never saw. He looks wildly at his sister, who is quite calm and looking about with perfect ease. He looks at me. Is there no force on earth that can protect him? Seemingly not! He draws in a huge breath as her great, ruined face descends, the lips pursing like in a drawing book, it is an ogre maybe trying to devour him, I do not know. But then a little miracle occurs.

'Oh, you are like Auntie Anne,' he says, with a sob of true relief. 'You have her cheeks, and her eyes!'

'Why, yes,' she says, 'I am her cousin!'

And suddenly the booming voice and booming body is changed to him. He holds out his short, thin arms and holds her fiery hair, and kisses her.

Then there is a kind of scattering, and a gathering, of old women, as May advances to take her share of the boy, and Lizzie and Winnie bestir themselves with the tea, delighted, redeemed like old blouses put to use again as polishing rags, marching out with loud clacks of their working shoes on the floors, coming back in with plates of sandwiches, thick-breaded things with mad slices of baked ham in them. Nevertheless they present no obstacle to the boy and girl. They sit at the soapy table and chew enthusiastically at them, smiling and laughing, the boy anyway, delighted with himself and his welcome. It occurs to me that the little girl must feel a touch neglected, such is the power and tide of a boy in such company. After all, they have seen and known enough of girls, being once girls themselves.

'Doesn't she have your hair, almost, Lizzie?' I say.

'She does, she does, she does,' says Lizzie. 'Or what it was before it did go grey on me!'

'Well, it is still nice hair,' I say, lying nicely in my teeth.

'Cack, cack, cack, cack,' says May, or something like it. Maybe the teeth that seem to have fallen out of her head have made her speech even worse than it was previously. She is tremendously excited. I can almost see the surges move through her. She keeps throwing back her head and laughing, and then trying to speak, and managing only, 'Cack, cack, cack, cack,' at which the little boy in turn tremendously laughs, but all in a highly agreeable way. We could be speaking of the stars in the most refined manner, such is the enjoyment of all.

At length I am able to leave the concatenation of the feast and take my chance to follow Winnie out, as she carries the kettle into the kitchen for a second fill.

It is a low, dark room, bare as the rest of the house, but for the cut-stone granite of the fireplace, very different to Sarah's but with the same arrangement of cranes and hooks. Everything is spotless, there is not a spider's web to its name. Winnie's hair actually scrapes along the old ceiling, which is curious.

'Matt's over in Lathaleer. Did you see him yet, dear?' she says.

'No,' I say. Matt in Lathaleer.

'He'll be over to you shortly, have no fear. He is mad after those two children. He is daft about them. He has boiled sweets bought for them, the ones they like, he says.'

'He hasn't been over yet,' I say.

'Isn't he only just down? Last night! Drove in that nice big car of his. Morris Major. And didn't it break down in Aughrim? Poor man. Got a jarvey all the way from there. Think of the expense of that!'

'Good for him.'

'Oh, unstoppable. He loves all that painting. Oh, he'll have been up since dawn now, with that easel of his, walking, walking, pausing here and there, like a fisherman.'

'Like a butterfly collector, my father used to say.'

'Did he, God rest him?'

I am glad that Matt's about again. Of course we don't get on. By rights he should keep away. Of course it won't be for me he comes visiting to Kelshabeg. It won't be for me. But this is not the question of the moment, no.

'Winnie, dear, there is a topic I wish to touch on, if I may?'

'I am so glad you brought them down, Annie. I don't know what I was expecting. City children. But they are lovely children.'

'Can I ask you something, Winnie — your advice on a matter?'

She changes her manner immediately, sets down the kettle, rests a hand on the table, looks at me seriously, gently.

'What is it, Annie? You look solemn.'

'It's — oh, God forgive me for not understanding the world sufficiently not to bother you with this, but. And I should likely say nothing. Let things take their course. Oh, and I don't want to make her unhappy, to wreck her chance of happiness, if that's what it is.'

'Who, who, who, Annie?' she says, like an owl in the sycamores.

'Sarah, Sarah Cullen!'

'What about Sarah? Her eyes, is it her eyes?'

'It is probably her eyes has her going the way she is going. And her age, and the pony and the tinkers . . .'

'Annie, Annie, hold your horses, what's the matter?'

I am trembling, sweating now in my summer dress. Winnie comes closer and puts her sisterly hand on my back. I can take no offence from that, though I am as always aware of the hideous hump in my spine. How close she puts her fingers to it. Touch not, touch not!

'What's the matter with Sarah, is she ill? Not that dreadful cancer that afflicts so many?'

'No! Thank God!'

I am astonished she has uttered the word, cancer. But it is the mark of Winnie. Even a shameful illness like that would not confound her.

'It is all Billy Kerr,' I say. 'Billy Kerr coming up to us, and talking to her, and I don't know what he has said to her, but it is all very strange. She says, she says they have an understanding . . .'

'Billy Kerr?'

She is very quiet for a minute. She is thinking.

'Well,' she says at last. 'Well, that is surprising, Annie, but I suppose people in general are surprising.'

'But, Winnie, is it not . . . is it not awful?'

'Awful? I don't know.'

'The ages, Winnie, are not right.'

'Oh? How old is Sarah Cullen now? I am sure she is sixty.'

'She is sixty-one, just a shade older than myself, two years between us.'

'Well,' she says, disastrously, 'Mrs Tomkin in the village was sixty-three when she married.'

'But Mr Tomkin was older than her, and it was his second marriage, after the first Mrs Tomkin died.'

'Well, I don't know, Annie. Billy Kerr is no spring chicken either. If he doesn't want children, it hardly matters what age his wife would be.'

'Spring chicken? Is he not forty-five then? I thought so!'

'Sure, no, no, Billy is in his fifties too. It's that we feed him so well, he looks like a gasur.'

'But, Winnie, Winnie, it's just the farm he wants, isn't it?'

'Oh, now, Annie, a woman with a farm is an attractive notion, but Billy Kerr, you know, he is very sincere.'

'Sincere?'

'Yes.'

She looks at me. I feel she can see into my worried heart. I feel she can read there after all the source of my fear. She looks at me I think with pity, biting her lip as she does.

'We are not against marriages, and we are not for marriages, ourselves. We never wished to marry here, you know,' says Winnie, leaning in to me, as if I have asked her that, but I haven't. 'Our father left the three of us the place. We would not divide it. We are happy to have each other. The first to die will be buried by two sisters, and the second to die will be buried by one, and the last will have to bury herself, and that is our story!'

And she offers her enormous, kindly laugh to the bare, scratched boards of the naked kitchen, and turns her back without insult and starts to heave the fresh-boiled water into the kettle.

Oh, I am surprised and disheartened by

her generous humanity. I thought I was so safe in my prejudices, and forgot the breadth of Winnie's sympathies. It is a disaster.

Chapter Eleven

As it is the boy's fifth birthday in July, it behoves me to carry myself whatever way I can now without the pony and trap to Baltinglass, and see if there is anything there in the haberdashery and general store that would interest a little boy. As it may be imagined, I proceed on my way with some grimness, after what Winnie has told me.

It is Pat Byrne the stone-man that gives me a lift in his Ford Anglia and I suppose he considers me a very glum package indeed in the bright red plastic seat beside him. But I cannot help it. I cannot hardly speak to myself let alone to him. I feel the world is against me and at the same time I feel miserably at odds with everything. I have the awkward sense that if I open my mouth people will know me for the villain I am. At the same time, or in the next breath, tears keep surging up into my eyes, tears of some righteousness, because my mind keeps rising to righteousness. All in all I am like a ragged wind in a tangled hedge.

Well, and I do find a highly suitable toy,

a wooden fire engine painted a fierce green.

This I carry back, entering the farm like a Russian spy, and hiding the present in its folds of newspaper under the hulk of the abandoned trap. I feel in my heart that it will make the little boy's head hot with pleasure when he sees it on the great day.

I am out of sorts now but not entirely so. The fire engine at least, I am thinking, is a victory of a kind.

Next day at evening time I am sitting on my three-legged stool, in the cow shed, milking Daisy and Myrtle. I can feel the hard little saddle of the stool against my hard backside. It is a marriage. Daisy has given up all she has, and now I lean in against Myrtle's warm bulk, to encourage her. I begin the little hauling on her teats, stretching them, squeezing them, and after a little, the warm milk starts to spurt, striking the zinc bucket with a satisfying ripping noise. This is work that would calm an evil God. Lucifer himself would find a balm in it.

The children come out to me, maybe scattered from the kitchen by Sarah. They stand in the wide doorway of the shed, darkening the interior a little. Myrtle pays them no heed. She thinks nothing of them, maybe, mere calves of human beings. Not that I really know how a cow may think. But she must be thinking something, to judge by the murky but intelligent eyes, the blue of mackerel. She is relaxed now, surrendered, or she could not give the milk.

They are holding hands, the boy and the girl. They are complete, content, sunburned. Their own eyes are bright as pebbles in the river, and they are giggling like friends. I have watched the little girl carefully but not seen hide nor hair of anything like the thing I witnessed. My worry about them is lessening. I am hopeful that it must have been a little experiment, a moment, one of those undesirable things that happen the once.

I have debated with myself whether I should ask the little girl about it, but I cannot find the words. I do not think she would know how to answer me. It would embarrass her terribly. Much as it offends me to think it, it must be a part of being brother and sister, a mimicking of love, I do not know. Despite what Sarah says, the little girl seems bright and whole to me now. She is full of laughter.

I bend Myrtle's supple teat towards

them and send a long stream of milk across the shed. The smell of milk bursts through the shed like a veritable seltzer, that odour of inside skin that babies too must have when they are born. It breaks up into a thousand droplets, glistening like mother-of-pearl. It cascades down and strikes the gansey of the boy, the dress of the girl. They scream with surprise and delight.

In the twilight of a few days following, I am carrying in a forkful of hay to Billy in his murky byre, when what light there is is erased by someone suddenly standing in the gap. I have been speaking to Sarah those days as if no catastrophe was imminent, because there is no other way we could continue to run the farm, and she falls I think gladly under the same foolish spell.

'I think this pony is getting fat,' I say. 'Maybe we should put him out onto the sloping field for himself, Sarah.'

'Maybe you should sell him, as I suggested,' says a man's voice, and of course it is Billy Kerr, who else? I do not feel entirely easy to have him standing in the light of the rough door. Billy the pony snorts and stamps on his smeared straw, which by rights needs mucking out.

'What do you want now, Billy Kerr?' I say.

'I want a word with you, Annie Dunne, as quiet as I can get it.'

'Oh?'

He steps in, releasing the few rags of daylight back into the byre. Billy's grey coat lightens a few shades. It is small enough for a pony, let alone a pony and two people, especially when one of those people, myself that is, would prefer now to disappear through the solid wall. I hate proximity, but proximity to a man whose voice is so sure and hard is deeply unpleasant.

'I suppose,' he says quietly, 'I could take you by the scruff of the neck, you old dog, and give you a mighty shake for yourself.'

'Billy Kerr!' I say. I am so shocked the blood is seeping out of my legs, it feels like.

'What are you trying to do to me?' he says. 'Going down to Winnie Dunne and having a go at me, like you did.'

'What I am saying to Winnie is none of your affair.'

'Is it none of my affair when the topic is myself? And you are making me out to be a blackguard?'

'A blackguard?'

'Don't play the innocent old woman,' he

says. 'Look it, here, Annie, I'll, what-cha-ma-call-it, enlighten you. Just so you will know and not be thinking you can do and say what you like around Kelsha and Feddin. In respect of myself. If you go about saying more, Annie, I'll come up here in the dark of the night,' and now he is very quiet, very quiet, 'and I'll do something to you — I'll hurt you, Annie, make no mistake.'

I am looking at him. Yes, a low person. Strength in his body from decades of labour. A dangerous, low aspect to him. There is a crouch in his shoulders I have noted before. He is clenching and unclenching his fingers like he wants to do this hurting to me now, without further warning. Should I say anything now? I am sorely afraid of him. His force and strength washes against me. He stands on the fork of his legs, pulsing, trying to convince me. He is convincing me.

'Do you understand me, you old bitch?'

'Do you think Sarah would let you talk to me in this way?' I say, without considering the words.

'How will she know how I talk to you? If you are saying anything to her, even a hint or whisper, I will twist your ugly old neck for you.'

Well, he is trembling with rage, I can see that. The twilight deepens in the yard outside, lending a strange dying vision to this talk. Somehow I feel like all my life is dying in the yard outside, all that I am, can be. Something is failing in my blood, in my heart, a measure of hope and female strength that has been there unquestioned throughout everything. It isn't just that I fear him, but that he feels able safely to offer me these speeches of hate and constriction. The word 'old' echoes and echoes among the four tottering walls of Billy's last refuge.

Then, oddly, something goes out of him.

'That's all I have to say to you,' he says, with some exhaustion. Maybe he thought he could achieve more, heave all opposition to one side with a great effort, and now the effort has drained him. Men are all sudden spurts and dashes. They do not have the long continuance of strength that women have by way of recompense. His face is not evil but it is ugly in the new shadows. And yet I know he is not an entirely ugly man. He is not stunted like so many of the men about, nor does he have that big red face that is so prevalent. He has been narrowed, even like myself, by the empty hand of possibility hereabouts.

Maybe the size, the emptiness of his ambitions exhausts him. Rattling in his hollow head. Now the blood pumps back into my legs.

'It's over my dead body you'll have anything to do with Sarah,' I say.

'Would you shut up about that? What are you talking about? I have said nothing to Sarah. I have said nothing to anyone. I am only going about my business in the countryside, I am only assisting and helping her, and you too I might add. Have you forgotten the ferocity of that animal there in the corner, and how I ripped the skin from my face leaping through a hedge of brambles for you?'

'My brother-in-law Matthew will be down shortly and he'll settle your hash for you, mark my words.'

'Matt? Matt hates you with whole-hearted hatred.'

'What?'

'Matthew? Maud's man? Are you crazy, woman? He is my friend. Of all you mad Dunnes and Cullens, he is my friend.'

'He is neither Dunne nor Cullen, and I tell you, if he thought you were about some unusual mischief here, he'd see to you, yes, he would.'

Now he is laughing, actually laughing.

'Are you a stupid woman, on top of everything else? With your nasty old tongue and that pitiful' — he forbears to say hump, but I know he wants to — 'pitiful long face of yours, Jesus Christ, years and years people have been putting up with you — do you think Winnie likes you, Annie Dunne? She does not.'

'But and she does.' But I wish I could be silent. Silence might stop him in his litany of truths.

'No, no. She thinks you are a rude piece of baggage, she told me so, just this morning, even as she was dressing me down, and threatening me with apocalypse if I . . .'

'If you what?'

'There's no one here in Kelsha likes you, no one. Why, Annie, Annie, do you think Sarah Cullen likes you?'

It is now very dark in the byre. Billy the pony is very quiet, he may be falling asleep on his legs, as is his wont. My soul is weary. I must be almost invisible. I hope I am. There are tears now, my own private tears that no one must see. When I was a little girl and my mother was dead, and my father, with all the responsibility of B Division and three little girls to raise, would in an extremity of rage shout at me, I would

221

hold good for the onslaught, but when he was gone, when he had stamped away in his police-issue boots, I would go into whatever cubby-hole I could find, and weep my private tears there. I am praying now for the new dark of the night to hide me, cloak me, preserve me. Maybe my father thought me hard and careless, I do not know. He never saw me cry. I owed my mother that, I owed him that.

'Hah?' he says. 'Hah?' He is like a hammerer of nails. 'Don't get in my way, Annie,' he says. 'I will skin you, I will take out your guts, I will take something you love and destroy it, that I will.'

'How do you mean?'

'How does anyone mean anything with you? You look down your ugly nose at me, but what are you? Little people that were once big people are all the more little now for that. And, if it was your father was the big noise, wasn't he a big, traitorous arse-licker to a foreign king? And what are you like here, only a serving woman? No, no — you do not even get a wage from Sarah. You are a slave, a slave to work.'

I have nothing now, only the hurried beating of my heart, I can feel it.

'And it isn't just that exactly, it is that no one in the world likes you. I never heard anyone say they did. You have nothing to recommend you. You go about here like you were something big, something grand.' He is laughing again, real laughter. 'And we're all thinking, that you're only a great gallumping pain in the backside, a stupid, bitter-tongued, wrong-headed, foul old woman!'

The little boy likes me, the little boy likes me. But it would be crazy to say that.

'You see, you see?' he says. 'You've to put all this in your pipe and smoke it. Because you are bringing trouble on my head. And I will not have it. I will not have an unloved, hunchbacked, mouldy old hag causing me grief! I tell you, I tell you!'

And in the smoke of his fury he is gone, gone away out, and I am standing there, his words that have leapt from the cauldron of his head now boiling in my own head, boiling, boiling.

It is difficult, difficult, it is difficult to stop my bones from breaking in their slings of muscles, to stop my head bursting. How dark and dirty the byre is. I think of the cleanliness of my father's world, polish and starch, everything in order, including hopes and dreams, including words themselves.

It comes upon me like a tidal wave that I

am a woman entirely alone, as if all these years in the aftermath of my father's life I have lived as if he too were living, somewhere, solidly, eternally.

All sorts of horrors strike me. In the moment of his death he was certainly alone, without even the attendance of those creatures that in their time ran the county home. Maud was so alarmed by his madness, in that to her it seemed a messenger of her own distress, that she would not accept the news that he was dead, and to Dolly it was only a piece of sad and distant news, where she nested safely in Ohio. And something gripped me too, some dread, some shame, some terrible stupidity, and I responded to the letter of the county home only weeks after, by which time they had buried him on the parish somewhere in Baltinglass, it being the very height of summer, and they were used, they said, to their inmates being, well, they said, left to fend for themselves.

And yet I had fended for him, going down Sunday after Sunday, though slowly gaps opened in those Sundays, of weeks, then months. He caused in me a terror too great to withstand, the long, wide body seeming to shrink down into that pale, old man with his broken thoughts and disturbing speeches. He could not remember my name half the time, but called me Dolly, and used to try and grip me in his weakened arms.

He died alone, and was buried as if in secret, like a hanged man, like one of those criminals he had dealt with in his forty years as a policeman.

And to this day I do not know where he is buried, my own father, because by the time I asked, their book was found not to record it, and the rough man who had attended him was gone, emigrated to Canada — so they said. So he lies now displaced and unknown in Baltinglass, in some weedy corner of some graveyard, without headstone or marker, an important man with responsibility for hundreds of souls reduced at last to less than a shadow, melting away for ever beneath the poor, municipal earth.

Because I did not bury him, somehow he did not die for me. He became again in my mind that healthy giant of my girlhood. I must have known well that he was dead, but my old brain, my dreams, my inmost thoughts, decided otherwise. And I have gone about for — it must be over twenty years — as if I still had his protection and the light, as one might say, of his position and his style.

But the words of Billy Kerr have knocked that weak notion clear away. Now I know I am alone.

It is like an emergency, like news of war, except the news comes from within the lost landscape of my own thoughts. And the war is somewhere there, across hill and down dale.

It is the next day and we are baking. I allow the little boy and girl to put the flour on the wooden table so we can bang and fold the dough there, and plump it into loaves. They delight in this, and return the delight into ourselves. Sarah carries a piece of the fire on the shovel out into the yard, where we have set up the pot oven for the loaves. Six we will make for the week, six loaves to measure the hours. It is as if all is right with the world.

The little boy is fascinated by the flour, the dryness of it, the cloudiness when he bangs his palms together.

'You're getting that all over,' I say.

He beats his hands down onto his legs and is astonished to see two hand prints there. He loads up his palms again and kind of leaps at me with a whoop, and slaps his hands onto my upper legs. It is reasonably painful, but he only wants to see the prints again on my blue and white apron. He turns then to Sarah.

'No, no, no,' she says, just settling the shovel again in its niche. 'Keep back with those paws!'

'Oh, Sarah,' he says. 'You must not escape.'

And he runs for her, and she skithers around the other side of the table with a mad screech.

The little girl cries out, 'Don't hurt her, don't you hurt that old lady!'

'Old lady, is it?' said Sarah. 'But I still have the gallop in me. He can't catch me.'

Round and round the table they go, the little boy eagerly holding out his hands, the flour flying softly from them. Against Sarah's prophecy, he does begin to catch up with her, and when soon she begins to run out of steam, he lands his right hand on her bottom with a smack. Sarah thankfully is laughing, the little girl is laughing, and now Sarah tries to stare back at her bottom to view the hand print, which further encourages the hysteria of the children. Then suddenly I feel myself being tickled on my sides, with the firm fingers of a grown-up, and I wheel about, and there is Matt, just in the door with his easel slung over his shoulder, laughing now loudly too. But I must admit the shock of this quite takes the laughter out of me. It is one thing to have him creep in unknown, another thing to see him at all after all our misadventures, and thoroughly another thing again to have him put his hands on me like that. I am put to silence and don't know what to say. The children alter their attentions in an instant, and fly to him.

'Papa, Papa, Papa!' cries the boy. He is altogether smitten, altogether made nearly daft with happiness to see his grandfather — who in his own fashion he calls Papa not Grandpapa.

Of course, he is a great favourite with the children. That is the way of things. Nevertheless I notice there is a part of me that is vexed by this vision of joy.

The little boy fires himself into Matt, and Matt laughs gratefully and holds the child to him, stroking the back of his head. Then he gleefully kisses the little girl, who is infinitely more quiet than her brother, but just as infinitely pleased.

'Giants,' he says. 'Giants.'

But he has the doing of these children every Sunday of the week, or used to before their father decided to make a go of it in London. Now here he is, gathering the nectar again. I am vexed, and I am sure he sees that I am.

How often in the past he saw it, in all the thousand rows we had, about the bringing up of his sons, about what to do with Maud and her moods, and about his hero De Valera, a strange hero indeed for a Corkman, who might have had the good grace at least to follow Michael Collins, but that was Matt all over. At least when Collins was killed, even a person like me could feel that sorrow, violent and devious though he was. Now De Valera was king of us all, and my heavens it seemed to be Matt's duty in the world not to let me forget it. But he had married the chief superintendent's daughter, head of the old Dublin Metropolitan Police, under the old dispensation, so whatever he said to me it was eternally true that his sons were the grandsons of that man, and carried him within themselves. This I never let him forget. All this flashes in my head in the seconds it takes for the tickles, the children, the greetings.

Now he dispenses the boiled sweets, drawing the two brown paper bags with gestures of glory from the pockets of his worn tweed jacket, with their characteristic leather patches on the elbows. And I am viewing his old shoes, leather again, beautifully kept, thick with polish, snug in a set of overshoes. And the canvas gaiters, and the trim crease in his thick trousers, and the thickly starched shirt, and the perfect knot of the tie, and the sculpted perfection of the trilby hat. It is all miraculous in a man, and I know no man like him. His hair, which is still thick and ruddy, is combed back in a kind of ploughland, with slightly sticky-looking ridges, and he is as shaved as a newly killed pig. What the men about Wicklow with their easy ways make of him I do not know, except Billy Kerr accounts him a friend, and I have seen him talking easily to people along the green road, especially to the wives, and he has never passed a woman of whatever degree without raising the same hat, although I notice on this occasion he has had no chance at all to doff it to us, if he was intending to doff it to us. And country wives, astonished by his manners, and by the apparent simplicity of the man, because he is no toff, but the son of a poor lithographer in Cork City, who when he died some years back bequeathed his son a pair of working boots that he had under the bed, 'hardly used' as he said to Matt. And Matt carried this trophy home, and put them by the fire in his studio, but never has worn them to my knowledge, but I did sometimes see him gazing at them, between strokes of the brush on whatever picture he was working at.

The children take the sweets like dogs to the edge of the group, and start to examine and eat them.

'There will be mighty long eating in them,' says Sarah.

'How are you, Sarah?' says Matt, now free to take off his hat.

'Oh,' says Sarah, and moves her head to indicate she's well enough.

'And Annie, how is Annie?' he says, turning to me.

'Annie is all right,' I say.

'How is the new missus?' says Sarah brightly. 'And when, when will we see her?'

'She is down with friends at the Strawberry Beds, at the minute,' he says, pronouncing 'minute' in his strange Cork way, *minyoot*.

'Friends from her days at Guinness's?' I ask blithely. Let no trace of bitterness intrude, at any rate.

'No, Annie. Her nephew lives by the Strawberry Beds. In fact, he is the curate to the parish priest in that part of the world. He is a very admirable young man. Fluent in the Irish.'

'Isn't that great?' says Sarah, a stranger herself to that language, unless Kelsha itself can be termed Irish, which I must suppose it is. Certainly the good nuns of the Loreto College in North Great George's Street didn't trouble themselves much with that old language of gobdaws and cottagers. Sarah's schooling as I remember, conducted in Kiltegan, was over by the age of twelve. But for Matt, who it seems fired a few shots in 1916 down in Cork City, and so must be termed a patriot, Irish is a holy thing, despite the fact that his half-brother was a chaplain in France in the Royal Irish Rifles during the Great War.

'It is wonderful to think that those two children will have the Irish when they are grown,' he says, accepting a cup and saucer from Sarah.

'I don't see how it will help them,' I say. 'What is wonderful about it? No one speaks it.'

'It is spoken, Annie, throughout the districts of the West, and some day it will be spoken again generally in Ireland. Isn't it our own tongue?'

'Not that I ever noticed,' I say.

'You are surrounded by things you never notice, Annie.'

'I'll thank you not to be rude to me in my own house.'

'I'm sorry, Annie. I wasn't being rude. I was being blunt, like yourself. You are one of that class of persons that can dish it out, but you can't receive it.'

'I can receive it well enough,' I say, with an eerie calm. 'What did you want to say to me?'

'Annie, can we put the loaves in the pot-oven?' Sarah says. 'I can smell rain. Did you smell rain, Matthew?'

He lets his easel down and sits at the far edge of the table, and drinks a sip of his tea.

'It hasn't rained for two weeks, Sarah,' he says, agreeably. 'Do you think it will suddenly rain now?'

'Go and put the loaves in, Annie,' she says, 'anyway.'

'All right, Sarah,' I say, and take up the three lumps of dough we have ready, and carry them out on their greasy tray. Outside the yard is a lovely bowl of warm sunlight, sweet and clear. There is about as much chance of rain as there is of gold falling from the sky.

Chapter Twelve

Every second day or so Matt comes to see us, bringing the past with him. That is how it seems to me. I cannot get out of my head all those years of work, raising the three boys in the place of my sister, who lay all the hours above in her bed, in the return of the house. She lay there for years amid the daytime songs of the blackbirds.

At the end of the garden was the monastery wall, and beyond that the monks paced their avenues, with their prayers and their secret thoughts. The huge sycamore opened and closed the doors of the seasons, letting in that miserly Dublin light in winter, doling it out in summer through its million singing leaves.

By the summer of 1950, when myself and the century were surprised to find ourselves fifty years old, the two eldest boys were almost grown — in a measure of time that seemed only the downturn of a sparrow's wing — lounging in the deck chairs in the back garden, with their outlandish beards, their queerly coloured suits and ties, watching their father fuss over his apple tree, his roses. It was one of those magisterial summers that come once in a decade, in twenty years, when all the rivers of the country run low and the old roads of these backwoods districts turn into whitened ribbons.

Matt was at war with his eldest son, at war with the greenfly. But he set a shining hubcap he had found on the Shelly Banks into the grass, for a birdbath, and he would go up to his studio on the first floor, and sit there for hours, drawing the birds that came to drink. And Maud alone a-bed throughout. What was wrong with her, the doctor could not say. She grew fat and sick and queerly happy there. At night, of course, Matt left us, entering that return bedroom, closing the door.

He had painted country scenes on the panels of his doors downstairs, and in the bathroom he covered the failed, foxed edges of the mirror with tiny, painted flowers. He read Dickens and Shakespeare in the fading light from his garden. He polished his shoes, and brushed his hats, and was grateful for his ironed shirts and trousers. In the deep reaches of the night, when I could not sleep, the eldest boy perhaps out on the town I knew not where, I would set up my ironing in the stove-warm kitchen. Eventually the boy would return, with his wild hair and eyes, exhausted, excited, uneasy. If Matt heard him entering the hall, the clicks of the door betraying him, he would come down all hissing anger and fear. Otherwise I gave the miscreant cocoa in my lair, and looked at the boy's sleepy face, and wondered what life he was leading. Was there true adventure in it, and was it all bravado, exhaustion and desperation? He was studying to be a sculptor at the College of Art. One day he brought home a beautiful wooden figure of Christ praying, which surprised us all. I had imagined wildness in his work too, scandalous things.

By contrast, his brother, the children's father, was all early nights and decency and thoughtfulness, making him the apple of Matt's eye.

I peeled the potatoes in the scullery, made the meals, scrubbed the tables, polished everything that could shine, brushed out everywhere, scoured, seared, ordered the larder under the stairs, killed the mice, banished the spiders, trapped the summer flies on fly paper, washed, dried, ironed, folded the clothes, the sheets and linens, went to my rest as tired as a wolf, as easy in my conscience as a lamb. It was a world for me, a sort of paradise, Elysium. I would lie in my bed thinking of everything, and I would dream of Matt, a strange dream where I opened his bones with a little saw and instead of marrow in them there was quicklime. In that dream then afterwards — how I put him together again I do not know — we would sit together in the dining room, side by side, the sunlight flooding down on our four knees. It was a queer little dream of peace and quietude, in which there was no Maud.

Then suddenly there was no Maud, the poor girl died, Maud died and there were frightening changes. The queen was gone from the heart of the realm, and I had not even known she was queen. Matt and I argued about everything, the very morning of her funeral we argued, when the eldest boy said he would not go. And it was then also in all honesty I noticed that he was in the upshot a tender boy enough, because the reason he would not go was plainly, his love for Maud was too great to bear the claptrap at the grave.

There was a sea change everywhere in that city household. My paradise was falling to perdition. Matt's eyes looked hurt and full of hate in the same instant. He would sit at the polished tea table, holding his face in his hands, dropping tears onto the bright wood. The eldest no longer came to sit with me in the kitchen, he stayed out later and later, until, in a great morass of fury between himself and his father, he slouched off to Spain.

Matt taught not just children their painting but also the odd grown-up student, the odd lonely spinster or man with an artistic bent. Someone called Anna started to crop up in his talk, such as it was. 'Tea with Anna' was the ominous phrase, in Lipton's or the Monument Creamery. I watched him go out and come in for a few months. I watched him, feeling more and more like a beaten dog. What had I expected? We were at each other's throats morning, noon and night. But still, but still and all. Can I confess it? I knew what the love of woman and man was, I had more than a hint of that, because — and I will not ask God to forgive me this, because he made us so — I desired that small, rotund individual of a man.

Ah but, then came his announcement:

'All right, Annie,' he says, 'and you will be as likely glad to hear me say this, considering, but I have asked Anna Smith to marry me, and I think that will mean you finding another berth.'

238

My marching papers and no mistake, nor no thank you either. Came then sorrow, and grief. I fetched about me, writing to this cousin and that, saying I would be happy to work my way for any bed they could give me, and put the few sixpences I had saved into hens or whatever I might.

At first I had a yearning to stay near the great city, and felt I might, and wrote especially to my cousins, the children of my father's brother, that kept the huckster's shop in Townsend Street, hard by Trinity College — their mornings full of fellas in those blue and red scarves, south Dublin kids. One of those children of my uncle had gone to be a priest, and was now, *mirabile dictu,* auxiliary bishop of Dublin, the Very Reverend Patrick Dunne, Bishop of Nara.

Let me tell a strange thing, but Nara is a district of North Africa, and I do not think the said Patrick ever has been to see his flock, but at any rate, haven't the bishops divided up the world for themselves like the Roman emperors did before them? I wrote to him too, when I was declined by his siblings in the huckter's shop, and he said to me that he had a fine housekeeper, was hoping I was keeping well, and please to remember him to Matt, and he would pray for me, and was of the opinion that God would bless me, as a good woman and a hard worker, and he signed himself with the very undignified name of *Pat*.

So, yes, briefly I cursed a prince of the church, and thought of that great palace of his in Haddington Road, and the number of empty bedrooms in it, and I hope the good natives of Nara will forgive me my blasphemous contempt. Finally, finally, I thought of Sarah Cullen in her little farm of seven acres, with six further acres of scrubby woods, and by heavens she wrote the most charming of letters on blue paper with red lines, and I remember it to this day:

Kelsha,
Near Kiltegan,
Near Baltinglass,
County Wicklow

7th September, 1957

Dear Annie,

It is Sunday and I am receiving your letter on Saturday by the Saturday post. Well, Annie, it was only in the summer I was thinking, when you were down in Lathaleer, just wondering and thinking would you ever want to return this way to Wicklow. And here you are now writing and asking, and asking the very thing I wish myself. Please now without hesitation, do pack your bag and get your ticket for the Wicklow bus, and come to me, because you will receive only the heartiest of welcomes, and be a proper boon to me.

> *Yours truly,*
> *Sarah*

The rescue of Sarah. And well I know the trouble the composition of that letter would have caused her, and the hours she must have spent that Sunday morning framing it in a way she would have liked to have it framed herself, to spare me the proper shame that Matt had put on me.

All these matters his presence brings back like a forceful fire. And now Sarah with her own threat of marriage. I do not understand it, I do not understand the nature of my fate, my ill luck, my true place in the world. It is not enough to be a slave to work. It is not enough to treat those around me with all the respect I can muster, and in Sarah's case, the love and affection I have for her. His presence in this time of frailty further reduces me with the recollection of past frailty.

And yet I would not forgo his presence. It seems to a part of me like enormous luck to have him in the district — no doubt, no doubt the foolish, fond part of me.

I do not care about Anna and try not to think about her. I lie beside Sarah in the night-time, sweating, in a fashion I never sweat. It is like I am unwell, but I do not feel unwell. I do not understand it. I think I do not want to understand it.

We are having a picnic up by the corn-stand, myself, the children and Matt, him in his tweed suit and polished brogues, all brown and green he is, the colours of the crab-apple. We are not twenty yards of the roofs of the house and outhouses, but we hold our picnic there because the little boy thinks the circle of cut-stones, that indeed do look for all the world like great big stone mushrooms, ten of them in a circle, he thinks they are something to do with picnics, and if not picnics, fairies. The little boy has an interest in fairies, though Matt is not a one to fuel that interest, Matt is practical, citified. No, it is a great-uncle of the boy's, a man called Pat O'Hara that was mayor of Sligo in Forty-two, an uncle indeed of the child's mother, who has told him all about fairies and fairy lore, not to mention the two-headed dog that he saw one night in the lights of his Ford on the Enniscrone road. I know the details of this because the child tells me over and over these matters, and forgets he has told me, and tells me again with all the freshness of a Biblical child recounting miracles, tales of a certain Jesus Christ just passed through his district. The boy loves and even reveres all his relations. I think he thinks we are nearer gods than mortals, it must be so. His grandfather, his mother's father, in his sailing days, the boy tells me, fetched into Liverpool one journey's end, took a room in a rundown boarding house, and was awake the whole night with someone sighing in the room, and betimes falling in beside him in the bed, but of course, when he lit his candle, not a soul was there to be seen. And he left that place in the morning, and heard much later that the landlady had murdered her husband, because he was found under the floor of that very room, as dry as the carcass of a mouse. These are the stories of a boy.

I am sitting on the chequered knee-blanket Matt has carried up from his car. I am sitting there, half watching the girl and boy as they climb the old stones. The corn right enough used to be set up on top of them, on a framework of beams, so the rats could not reach the grain while it dried in the natural ovens of summer. Matt is talking to them, now and then brushing stray stalks from his trousers, laughing, talking, shooting the breeze he calls it, and indeed shooting his starched cuffs into the bargain. I suppose he is a dandy of sorts, what the wily local men might call a bucko. He despises the English or rather hates them as the old enemy of his youth, yet in the same breath of fact, isn't he as close to an Englishman as makes no odds? He is more like the class of character a person might see issuing forth from Humewood in the old days, when there was still money and guests, and the old lady there was not inching quite so into decrepitude, along with her many-roofed mansion. The only thing flourishing there now I imagine is the rot in the roof beams, God help her, though there was a time naturally when pennies to her and her family were like rain in a filthy season, ever descending on them.

Curiously enough, there is a touch of my

dream about it, because the sunlight is sitting on my knees through the thin cloth. I have that knee-warm feeling. I have many feelings, I suppose, turning all on the same sixpence. Sunlight, sunlight, there is ease in it, if no future, no guarantee of being there tomorrow. It is a moment of ease, of nice laziness, Matt cavorting now, on his own knees, indifferent to the grass stains, giving horse rides to his niece and nephew. The eggs that Sarah has boiled for us lie in their strange pyramid on the opened handkerchief she had wrapped them in. The sweetened water sits in its heavy earthenware jug, juggling, one might say, the very sunlight on its surface, a little splay of blowing and fading stars. Deep in the warm trees there will be animals, badgers asleep, foxes in their short cuts. Bullfinches, blue-tits, yellow-tits, mere sparrows, cascade at the corners of the picnic, where we have thrown our crumbs. If Matt is happy, the children are delirious.

Eventually, panting and hot, Matt sits down beside me. He chooses a boiled egg and sinks his white teeth into it, white against white, though different whites they are.

'Papa, Papa, Papa!' cries the little girl. 'Don't sit down!'

'I must, I must,' he says. 'I am dying.'

'Don't sit down like Auntie Anne,' says the boy. 'Don't sit down like a grown-up!'

'Oh, thank you,' I say.

'But I must,' says Matt, 'or I may die!'

Nothing then for a little. I am tempted, sorely tempted to peer beside me at his knees. Does he feel yet the influence of the sunlight? Is there warmth gathering there?

'This is one spot in the world,' he says, 'where Magritte might find an answer to his paintings.'

'Who is that, Magritte?' I say.

He does not even look at me. Why would he bother? I do not actually know what he is talking about. But I remember the rows he had with his eldest son over such strange names, the misery it caused them both, shouting, and doors banging. Although that son was an artist too and should by rights have been of like mind.

Then he says nothing a while, letting the sunlight stew along his clothes. The friendly smell of tweed rises from him. Single flies whine across us, firing off into the woods. That ease beyond price that is in the gift of summer has seeped into my marrow. Co-co-co-rico goes the wood pigeon, the only thing that it ever says, that it never tires of saying.

'Realism, you see,' he says, like another normal person might comment on the weather. 'Ah well.'

He is dark to me really. I'm looking at him. An Irishman of middle years, of later years, a painter, teaching drawing to rascals of boys in the technical school in Ringsend, smiling out at the view. The woods above us are very dark too, despite the brightness of the day. To the best of my knowledge he is not known among artists. Yet he is at ease now, polished, starched, happy somehow. I must remember the strange name. Magritte. So I can talk to him sometime about these matters that preoccupy him. Magritte.

Suddenly, in the midst of all that peace, not least this peace between Matt and me, I want to ask about the children, I want to have his views on what I witnessed — to release me from my doubts and intimations, so I am no longer alone with them. Even the night before as I lay in bed, when a person is prey to fears, a strange thought came creeping into my mind. The thought was but a shadow, a hint. Something about Trevor, the little girl, a notion I could not make clear to myself.

'They do seem happy,' I say.

'Oh yes,' he says.

'The girl has settled in,' I say lightly, but inviting, I suppose, a comment.

'She is happy as a sunbeam. Children that age are always happy.'

I hesitate. The seeds of dandelions bump along in the air. The little boy is puffing at the soft, round heads, laying them waste. One o'clock, two o'clock, three o'clock . . .

'Trevor loves them dearly, of course,' I say.

'What do you mean, Annie?' he says, his face coarsened with puzzlement. 'Trevor adores them.'

'Yes. Yes, he does.'

He catches something in my tone, or so I imagine. At any rate, he is looking at me now as if I were that two-headed dog on the road to Enniscrone. Now it is him who doesn't understand me. I am afraid to say anything further, but I must.

'I caught the little rascals kissing the other day,' I say, with a false laugh. My cheeks flush.

'Ah well,' he says. 'Did you never practice your kissing as a little girl? I suppose you didn't.'

Oh, why do you suppose that? Why, Maud and myself practised kissing till our lips were sore, in the privacy of the back scullery in our castle quarters.

'Kissing!' he says. 'Quite natural, quite natural, Annie.'

He is the father of three boys, he must know. The wonderful flavour of the day reasserts itself. It is like Eden, my own father used to say, in the bright dispensations of the summer months. These days that, even as you live through them, seem like memories, caught up as they are in the lost happinesses of other, similar days.

He gives a little laugh, and takes his gaze off me, as if he thinks I am mad.

'You know, Annie,' he says, leaning back on the grass, chewing at his egg — already he has put the matter out of his head — 'you are doing a wonderful job with these children. They are as active as chimpanzees. How do you do it? I wouldn't last a day. They are lovely, oh yes, but, heavens you would need to be in the first flush of youth for them!'

'You have to know how to manage them,' I say, a little dizzy now with relief, 'like any other creature — how to farm them, in effect. Though, yes, there are nights when Sarah and I fall into bed with the gratitude of women reprieved.'

'Well, I hope Trevor is good and grateful, and I'm sure he is.'

'Well, we have heard nothing since he

left to go. The little boy writes a scrap of a letter to him every day. Just scribbles and gobbledegook. I am keeping the letters. But I am hoping their father will write soon, or I will have to make up a letter, and pretend it's from him.'

'And their mother?'

'Oh, just the same.'

'They will be very preoccupied, setting up house.'

'Oh, yes.'

'And they are safe here. They know that. Nowhere safer than Kelsha and Annie. You are doing a tremendous job, tremendous. Yes, I am saying to you, Annie, I am admiring you for it.'

So I am silenced by that, how could I not be? It is praise from on high — I almost said, from the master. I luxuriate in it, I confess. For those moments I feel like the greatest minder of children, the greatest great-aunt that ever lived.

'Ah, sure,' I say, 'it is a pleasure mostly.'

'They are grand children,' he says, watching them. 'Grand.'

What I would like to say to him is, 'Matt, Sarah too is on the brink of marrying. What will I do, what will I do? Who will take *me* in, and guard me, and be father and mother to *my* fears? Won't you help me, Matt? Won't you take me back?'

But pride, oh, and sense too, forbids it. Of course it does. I know the story of the world. Aching hearts and silences. So was it ever, so will it ever be. I must be tremendous Annie instead, on the dry grass as near to fire as makes no difference.

Oh, grind up the furze-root as you might, and feed it to us, you could not put the two of us a-ploughing. Grind up the furze, grind up the furze, but I fear it will be to no avail!

When he is going out the gate that evening, I give him a wrap of my butter, as a memorial of the day. He says he will spread it upon his bread in the morning, under the heats of Lathaleer.

And like old friends fond of each other's company, we make a plan for one of the days to drive in his Ford into the Glen of Imail, and choose some wild spot there with the children, and picnic again.

Strange days of peace, considering.

That evening I play with the children with an odd abandon. It is the game they love, *How Many Miles to Babylon?* They take turns, dutifully, but with ferocious desire in their eyes.

I put the little girl up on my knees for

251

the umpteenth time. My lap is sore and rubbed by them. My old dress has taken a drubbing. But, what do I care?

'How many miles to Babylon?
Three score and ten.
Will I be there by candlelight?
Sure, and back a-*gain*.'

And when I reach the *gain*, I let her down suddenly between my legs, holding her hands, her scream echoing in the lime-washed room. The little boy is already jumping and clamouring for his go. Sarah is laughing in the shadows.

Candlelight, candlelight.

Chapter Thirteen

An old woman, one of the O'Tooles, that lived in the last house except one on Keadeen — the rabbit man is the last — has died, and Sarah has gone up the mountain road to lay her out. She is a woman I never knew, and abided her last days in a tiny thatched cabin with mud walls, all half sunk back into the wild earth from which it was made. How lonely she will have been. Neighbour she had none, except the rabbit man. And he is a man of few greetings mostly. The odd time there is the summer of talk in him. But when you might see him on the road betimes, and when that usual mood is on him he will barely greet you. And when you turn your head again to see him, he will be gone, gone out of sight entirely, plunged up silent and quick into his woods, like a spirit, like a vanishing sprite.

So that old woman cannot be said to have had a neighbour.

I did not even know she was there until her family came in and asked for Sarah. For Sarah is always called on for the laying out, and when she was younger, and a child was sick in a neighbour's house, oftentimes she was sent for, for to suggest a remedy. Of course there is the good doctor, Doctor Byrne, but he must have money for his work. Sarah will take no money, nor nothing else in kind. It is a part of her secret, a reclusive gift.

But I notice these years she is never sent for. It is to do with the tarring of the roads, the demise of the traps, the death of things we knew in general. A gift like hers is no longer trusted, being a home-made thing. The shop-bought bread, the shop-bought medicine, it is all part and parcel of the same thing. At least now, when a last woman is to be taken from the mountain, where she must have lived in secret penury, the family have the justice and the ceremony to call on Sarah.

She has gone up the hill with her candle, her basin and her cloths. She will wash that old lady for the last time, and burn the clothes after at the back of the midden. She will lay those cool cloths along arms and withered legs, she will scour out the old body, and plug her gently, and fold those arms of long work and toil. If she was a child of Mary at school as a little girl, she will have a blue habit folded in a drawer and Sarah will put that on her, as a mark of her goodness, or at least, former goodness. If there are scapulars sewn into her knickers, she will snip them out and give them on to the eldest girl among her surviving relatives. They are all people that have left this district. Her great-uncle was the famous silent man, Wesley Mathews, who spoke but seldom. It is said that when he went to America he was conversing with a neighbour on the last day. The neighbour says to him, 'Wesley, see that blackbird. It is the blackest blackbird I ever seen.' Wesley said nothing, but went to America the next day. Fourteen years later he returned, and met the neighbour on the road. 'It is,' he said.

But that is a story told about many places, and it may have no truth. Sarah will not be thinking of such a thing while she works.

Then poor Father Casey with his onerous gout will come up past us here in his car, driven by his man German Doherty, humming no doubt one of his dancing tunes. Because German Doherty plays in the ceilidh band, and after the harvest they are called on to visit the houses, when people want dancing and happiness. He cuts a sharp figure there with the priest, German Doherty does. They will sweep up the mountain, German dodging the worst of the ruts in the track, and singing. Then that old woman will get her oils and her solemn prayers. At the close, Sarah will place a candle in her hands, and open the window. And when the wind blows out the candle, that will be called the fleeing of the soul, up to the heavens.

God forbid that Sarah should ever have to lay me out. That would be a short walk for the work, from her side of the bed to mine.

So I am left alone in the house and must shoulder Sarah's tasks. It is a taste of the life she has led before I came, a list as long as a pig's intestine. You can make a lot of sausages from the one pig, if you have the stuffing. I remember my father delighting in the slaughter of the pig, the cutting, and then, him in his hobnail boots walking on the carcass, to work the salt into the skin. Such food would bring my father fiercely up the yard, if he knew there was a wodge of cured bacon cooking. And truly it is a magnificent food. The skin all salty and tender because of the walking, the flesh all pungent and wild as brambles because of the boiling.

Often and often Matt carried me over in the Ford to see my father while he languished in the county home in Baltinglass. In truth it was the workhouse of old, and these days they are wanting to call it not even the county home, but the hospital. They can call it what they want, but it is still a bleak, dark house of granite stones, and in a room of that place, a veritable cell, my father descended, losing wits and sense, and even his clothes, which he gave away near the end to another man, a hero of his youth also incarcerated in that spot. And in I went one day and found my father in his long johns! I did not laugh, though I almost laugh now to think it. I suppose I did not see the humour then, because in truth there was none. It was all too bleak, such a resplendent man, with his uniforms, his bulk, and his habit of command, as he called it, reduced to an ember of that fire, one coal in the grate, one fragment of coal, barely showing in the darkness. 'Annie,' he would say to me, 'Annie, where's Dolly?' and I would tell him she was in Ohio, and then half a minute later he would ask again, and I would tell him again Ohio, and he would look at me as if it was information he was getting for the first time. And I do not know how they treated him in that place. You never know what happens after they shut the doors on you, and they have the old inmates to themselves. I forget the man's name that tended him, but he was a dark bull of a man from Cavan or somewhere the like uncivilized, and I did not like him.

There was no one there when he died. There was not. I do not even know who laid him out, who blessed him, who lit a candle for him and opened the window to let out his soul. He had less in that way than this old dame upon Keadeen.

I hope God will forgive me, I do hope he will. I hope St Peter will let me pass the gates.

I am thinking these thoughts and I have finished banking the fire and giving the flags a sweep and flicking the feathers at the crockery. So I wander out through the half-door to escape the little storms of dust. The little boy is playing there, at a game of childhood in the shadow-hooded yard. The sun now climbs down Keadeen, her lights have lifted and lie on the slates of the calf byre, like golden slates themselves. Such an old, humble place, with such a wealth of gilding! But what is the boy playing with? There is something green under his foot, and he is skating on it, but in a stumbling manner, down the middle gutter of the yard, where the ground is smoother and flatter, to fetch off the rain-water when required.

'What have you found there, child? Is it a piece of wood?'

He visibly gives a start, his short round shoulders jumping. He turns his head slowly to look at me, the brown eyes as hooded as the day. He looks both fearful and angry, I cannot say it plainer. I have never seen such a look in him before.

'What have you got there?' I say, and proceed over to him, feeling suddenly very like my poor father, approaching what seems very like the guilty party.

I reach him. I look down at the object under his foot. He looks down at it, and then back up at me.

It is the green fire engine I have bought and hidden in the barn for his birthday. The wheels hang out at the sides, quite forced and ruined. The half-dry mud of the gully, that probably in all truth carries also the urine from the calves in the shed, has smeared the gift, turning it from that bright fresh toy into an aged thing. It is only good now for laying out itself. I stare down at the boy's face. Yes, a filthy anger rises in me, something prompted by his own look, his demeanour of misery and defiance.

'Where is your sister? Would she not have prevented such — such brutality? Such thuggery? Have you gone into the barn and took it out? Are you so brazen, so wild, so cruel?'

'I was in looking for eggs for you,' he says. 'I put my hand in a shadowy place and found it.'

'And do you know what it is?'

'It is a green fire engine.'

'But why do you think it would be there in the barn?'

'For fires,' he says. 'For green fires.'

'It,' I say, lifting his foot off the toy, and lifting the toy from the gutter, 'is your birthday present.'

He basks me in a look of entire joy. But I crush that joy under the heel of my stare.

'It was your present,' I say. 'For it is no more. Now you have no present. Now I have gone to Baltinglass and spent a month's money on this joke, and now it is destroyed, and you will have no surprise.'

Of course, even as I allow my anger rein, like Billy the pony himself, I know it is not him who will have no surprise, but me who will have no pleasure in fetching the present in to him, on the bright morning of his birthday. He was born in the great heatwave of 1955, and therefore owns a sunny disposition. But my words strike harsh clouds across his eyes, I dim his lights for him. I can see it. I can feel it. But it does not stop me. I know I am murdering him, because I understand the small language of his looks. Never have we stood against each other like this. The smaller voice inside me cries out, mercy, grant him mercy, Annie. But some other loud, vicious, uncontrollable thing calls.

I am as near to striking him, even to kicking, as puts a true fear into me. I march away with the engine instead, and past Billy's dark prison, and through the gables along the 'lane', and up to the dung heap. I place the engine on the ground, and shove my hand sin-deep amid the rotting stuff, and tear away at the layers and lumps, deep as I can go, deeper, far deeper than the child could go, deeper, far deeper than will have it ever found again. I pray that the moisture of the dunghill will seep fast into its soft wood, and rot it, render it, reduce it like bones and skulls. Down into the morass I thrust the engine, and cover it back over with the muck. My arms smeared with odorous browns and greens from the elbows to the fingertips. And my head is racing, tumbling, painfully tumbling.

The little boy has not moved. He can see me well enough from where he stands. Then slowly he turns away, like a little monk, and walks gradually back to the half-door, and in he goes like the shadow of a hen. Red Dandy struts with her sisters in the upper yard. The sunlight kisses the ridge tiles of the calf byre. Everything is normal in the yard, everything in its place, except the misplaced anger of my heart, the topsy-turvy kettle of my heart, spilling out venomously onto the enrichened grasses.

Immediately the anger abates. Immediately I am guilty, with a dark, bladed guilt. I have given way to an ungovernable anger with the child I love. I am as ruined and smeared as the engine. I am destroyed.

She stuck the penknife in the baby's heart,
Weile, weile, wáile,
She stuck the penknife in the baby's heart,
Down by the river Sáile.

'You are upset, Annie,' Sarah says that night in the bed, her generous task for that old woman done. Her mind is on other things, on death and washed bones. She has listened to my tale of the fire engine, but with a withering interest. 'You are upset because of what I have put to you. Now when the boy does something as any boy would, that is in the nature of boys, you will be for going to war with him. I blame myself. I am sorry, Annie. The ball of twine is all twisting up. It was as neat as a newborn foal these two years. Now it is all twisted up.' Then she falls again to thinking.

I am silent too. I cannot speak to her. The little boy I sent to bed early, and the little girl for good measure. There are weights on my arms and my legs. I am weighed down, I am old. I cannot manage these two children. They are bringing me to distress. It is all an error on the part of their father. How could he think to leave them here, with me and Sarah, and all the years there are between us? What foul little instinct is it in the boy to fetch out the beautiful present and destroy it? To muck it up and make nothing of it?

Oh, I am festering. The starched sheet lies to my chin. Oh, but she is right. She is a wise woman. She is offering truth. But the truth she offers sticks in my throat like boiled spuds. I need a drink of milk to wash it down, but what shall this milk consist of? Some glean of sense, some descending peace. I must lie as still as a cat. I must wait for ease. That I might think, that I might think . . . More difficult for a rich man to enter heaven than a camel to pass through the eye of an needle. But more difficult still, a foolish, moiling old woman.

But the next day I feel I might have the remedy. If Sarah is correct then another effort must be made to avert what threatens me. I cannot stand day after day on the edge of the pit that Billy Kerr is digging for me. It would be foolish. Suddenly I remember that Matt is a friend of Billy Kerr's, or so Billy Kerr has claimed. Cannot he speak to him?

All day I wait as patiently as a salmon fisher for a salmon. I do not send for Matt, which would be an awkward action, but somehow I imagine and assume that he will be up the road to us, as has become his wont. I am not so blind as to think he comes for me, it is his grandchildren that he cannot get enough of. He paints about the countryside all the mornings, rising I know with the cockcrow and then sun, then no doubt he feels his footsteps drawn to Kelsha. Time afflicts him as it does the rest of us. Maybe he is thinking of that, the cramped space that we are given to be children in, how bright and brief it is. Now is his chance to drink the waters of their love for him. Oh, well he knows it, and well he ought to know it. Woe betide the person who does not.

And yet he does not come. We pass through the tasks of the day and there is no sign of him. The summer dark comes late against the hills, the yard closes over again, the hens are fed in the flashing shadows, Billy gets his share of hay in his pitchy byre, the children are folded in again to find their sleep. Has he gone about the countryside like the gleaners of old, making his quick sketches like a poor man collecting the fallen ears of corn, gathering the beauties of Kelsha, Feddin and Kiltegan, and then returned all tired and content to his bed in Lathaleer, and never a thought for me? I expect so.

If the little boy was gravely offended, the mercy of his age soon lightens him. A boy of nearly five cannot hold a grudge. I have a vision of him skating on the engine, he no doubt for a little while of me shoving the engine into the midden of muck. My vision abides, but his fades quickly. By mid-morning, after his egg in a cup, his soldiers of bread, he is as good as before, gentle and sweet, smiling and true. So we imagine we do them no harm by our crude actions. But I wonder. I wonder. For I remember now the slights of childhood, now that I am growing old and older, and sometimes they are bitter and large in my mouth. I remember how the girls of the Loreto Convent in North Great George's Street jeered my back, how I was never a girl among girls, but only a wounded creature among the complete. How straight were all their limbs, how neat their blouses hung on their spines. In the dark of my room in the Castle those straight backs would float above my bed, in their summer blouses. Even the ugliest face in the school could claim a pretty back. Backs were all my study, old women in the street, the young, the poor, the wealthy in their furs.

And when now and then rarely I saw another bowed-back girl, all my instinct was to jeer her too, although I had no licence to. This afflicting music of my childhood was hard to hear then, but I o'ercame it. It is now, oftentimes lying these decades later on a flattening mattress with a ticking of old goose down, that I am gripped by fearsome rages, to think of it. Never kissed, never fondled, never embarrassed by a boy's desire! It is a wretchedness.

Truly it is said, the child is father of the

man, or mother of the woman, in my case.

So wrongdoers against children should not imagine their crimes are forgiven, just because the child heals quickly before their eyes. The wound seeps down like a drowned person. Many years later it will bob up again to the surface, frighting the districts all about. This I know, this is my caution.

The next morning early I betake myself to Lathaleer, hoping to find him there. It is not a house I relish going to, because it was there my father endured his last days of freedom, as one might say, and that I tended him in the closing infirmity of his mind. He had been delighted to have the renting of it, that time his life as a policeman was at last over, and he was obliged to make some fist of a retirement. But forty years he had been among the men of the DMP, as recruit, as constable, as sergeant, as inspector, all the ranks even as far as chief superintendent, the highest rank a Catholic could hold. Commissioner was the only rung above that, and that was reserved for some English politician, and, truth to tell, a commissioner was rarely sighted and did no work that I know of. In my father's time also I remember there was not anyone to fill that job, so he was *de facto* the head of the Dublin police.

But Dublin at length became a ferment of murder and discontent, and his last days were spent among the insults and wounds of revolt and revolution. That great change in things I do believe hurt his simple mind. He could not rise to the new dispensation, he could not get crowns and kings out of his head, and give his loyalty to common gunmen, the sort that came in after and called themselves leaders.

His wits were sundered in his head. He sat in Lathaleer, the prospect of which had given him such initial joy, and felt even the scratchings of the mice and rats as things against him, the sough of the wind as an army of murderers. I could not hold that old humpty-dumpty together. The ropes that bound his skiff to the land of sense unravelled before my eyes.

Lathaleer was a site of sore suffering for me and him, and the poor end of it all was him bundled into Matt's car on a wicked, cold Sunday, and driven down to the county home like an old bullock sent straight to the glue factory, there to be rendered down slowly by the havoc of his mind and the indifference of his keepers. And at last, the cowardice of his daughter.

Oh, well I know it. And God will curse me for it at day's end.

In the upshot, Matt is not there. I wonder why I have been so foolish as to imagine he would be. He has gone out early as usual, the girls there tell me, and as he has brought a parcel of bread and butter and cheese — my butter I hope — they do not expect him back till late. I suppose that strange fever of making is upon him, when everything else passes to the second place, and all he desires is the next intoxication of fields and hills and riverlets, of browns and greens. It is an obstacle to my purpose, at any rate, although he still might wander in to us in Kelsha, so I turn back for home.

To reach the road going up to Kelsha, I must of course pass the stile leading in to the farm at Feddin. I fear this now for present reasons, as being infected by the presence of Billy Kerr. His insults are still loud in my head. But once a thought is in the mind, to cause some change in things, once the courage has been found to make the heave, it is hard to let it go by just because a man is about the landscape painting. Do I really need Matt to address the problem of Billy Kerr, when I might be as well to enlist again the assistance of Winnie?

Something in my inner heart bids me go on, to pass those gates and take the green road to Kelsha, but alas I crush that small instinct, and climb the stile, and make my way along the verdant avenue of buttercups and bell flowers. The musky heat hangs under the old oaks, the mothy ash trees. The yellow buttercups blaze like butter pats. The ground is dappled like a cowhide.

'God bless all here,' I say, as I cross their threshold and enter the wooden hall. There is no one there, no sound in the house at all, except the anxious beating of the grandfather clock, half done in by mildew and mould. Indeed the panelling I can see is suffering, buckling out from the water in the walls behind it. The sunlight peers in in a dusty column, revealing these secrets, like the hand of a stranger in the possessions of an old woman. For the house is old and female. There is a cleanliness to it, but also a suffering, a decay behind the front of things. I pass on through the parlour, silent as the hall, the table where we were given our tea and our salad, bare and scrubbed. They must be away out, at their tasks. I put my head around the door of the kitchen just to check. There is Winnie, with her reading glasses on her nose, and she would be reading the Wicklow paper, except she is sleeping. A bowl of sunlight cowls her round. She looks old but content, far, far more content than myself. She has a farm and sisters and a strong man to drive her about the place in the trap, and dig, and build walls back up when they tumble. She is rich in certitude, in affections, in place. I do not want to trouble her again. I go back out to the hall, tiptoeing on the creaking boards. They dip under my shoes, springy and strange.

'It's you, Annie,' says Winnie, now standing in the door behind me. 'Why are you creeping away?'

'Oh, Winnie, I did not wish to wake you.'

'I was only napping. Forty winks. It is the sunlight. Did you want to talk to me? Come back in, dear, sit down, have a glass of water for your thirst.'

I do as I am bidden, quite like a child. Winnie is not much older than me, but her manners are more a parent's than a cousin's. I sit in the chair allotted, an old child.

'I hope you did sort that out with Sarah.

I know how hard these matters of — whatever you might call it, can be. I never had such troubles myself. But I have been thinking about you. I spoke to Billy. He was very feeling. He is considerate. He promised to take due care, to steer a happy course if he could. Did you speak to him?'

'I did,' I say, remembering the torrent of curses. 'I — I wish you would speak to him again.'

'There might not be any use in going over the ground again. I think he will not disadvantage you if he can help it. Of course, it is for Sarah to think of too.'

'I cannot stand in the way of Sarah.'

'No, no, I wouldn't counsel that you do!'

'Of course not, Winnie. No, but if you could speak to Billy Kerr.'

'There's not much more to say to him. You know, if we lost him, there would be hardship in it here too. He has a strong and willing back!'

'I know.'

Now here's Billy Kerr in the kitchen door. I am suddenly afraid. I am creeping about right enough in the plans of the living, me, a half-dead person without rights or land. I am like those landless people that the hunger of the last century destroyed, creatures that could brook no change, without the consequence of their demise. Like Simeon, I would like to see the coming of the Lord before I die, but I will not even see John the Baptist, as the saying goes. Billy Kerr, all force and smiles, stands in the door. Such a smile he has, beaming at Winnie and me. He crosses to the water bucket, the surface still knocking about from the dipping of the ladle to quench my own thirst.

'I am beaten by the thirst,' he says, and dips the ladle, pours the liquid into a chipped cup, and drinks it down gladly, as if gladly. 'So, Annie,' he says. 'What brings you to us today, this fine morning?'

To us. How is it he vexes me so? Vexation upon vexation! And yet it is *us.* Because Winnie does not baulk at the word, and Winnie is queen of Feddin. Without bothering to wait for an answer, he says, 'The two sisters are up by the Humewood boundary, knocking the hell out of those brambles. Such women they are, with a slash hook. I never saw such swipes. They are like devils possessed.'

'We hate brambles, generally,' says Winnie, laughing.

'Well, that's quite clear!' he says. What pleasantry, what ease. I hate this man. If I could kill him quietly, I think I would. I would like to cleave his breastbone with a slash hook, now slash hooks are the topic, and reach into his ribs and put my fingers round his vigorous heart, and tear it from what tethers it.

'I was only passing,' I hear my small voice say.

'What's that, Annie?' he says, pausing and looking at me.

'You asked me a question. I was just passing, is the answer.'

'She was just passing,' says Winnie, smiling.

'Did I?' he says, and looks away again, and strides from the room.

'You see,' says Winnie. 'He has nothing against you. He bears no grudge.'

'Why would he?' I say.

'Well, a man doesn't like to find someone standing in his way. A man is like a flooding stream. He will leap the rock.'

'I am not trying —'

'You are not trying to stand in his way. I know.'

Oh, now the tears come. It is the motherly tone. So long ago since there was that tone to guide and comfort me.

'Oh, Annie . . .' she says, and crosses the red and black tiles of her comfortable kitchen. She stands beside my chair and puts a hand on my shoulder. This time I do not flinch away. I care not a jot now for bowed spines and hunchbacks. For that is what I am. How easy and nicer to say *bowed.* Cupid's bow indeed, something springy and useful. A bowed back. Almost a pretty phrase. Hunchback, hunchback is what you are. The hunchback of Notre Dame. The hunchback of Kelsha.

At length I bring myself and my tears away. Winnie comes to the door and, by grace of her concern for me, she hugs me briefly as I go. She passes back into her house, no doubt to resume her seat, her paper reading, maybe lightly to think on my visit, my dilemma, I do not know. So lonely and wretched I feel.

Billy Kerr leans against the big hay shed. He is smoking, idle. I glance at him, and my eye is caught by his eye. His face does not smile, he does not speak. I am so surprised by the aspect of menace in his slouch, in his lack of expression, that I actually stare. Is it really him, or is it a stranger? My long vision is not what it was, though not nearly akin to Sarah's. Both near and far vision are going with her. I have a horrible picture of her groping blindly towards Billy Kerr, in our bed! Banish such things, Annie Dunne! I almost think of calling for Winnie, such is my expectation of him speaking, or attacking me. He has roused the full measure of menace in himself, or so it looks from that distance. It is blurred, it is blurred. And then I think he is raising a hand, with the pointing finger extended, and he is wagging it at me, like a schoolteacher. That I do not imagine. I take myself off like a fox that hears the hounds as yet hidden behind the hills.

Chapter Fourteen

When I reach our farm at Kelsha, I pass up
the deserted yard. There is an upturned
bucket out of its proper place that I must
tend to, I notice. I see the children playing in
the sloping field, rolling and rolling. The
best days of their lives, simple days. But
Sarah is like a flame in the kitchen, dancing
here and there.

'You will not know what has happened,'
she says. 'Poor Matt, poor Matt.'

My first thought is, he is dead. Then an
emotion larger than a horse invades me.
Sorrow flashes along on its lightning lines,
jagged, painful spears behind the eyes. My
arms ache with a sudden emptiness. It is
very peculiar and confusing. In the next
moment I am angry.

'What has he gone and done to himself?'
I say.

'Will you be vexed about this too,
Annie?' she says.

'He is a man to make anyone angry,' I
say. 'Bumbling about. Well, well?'

'He was somewhere at the edge of
Kiltegan painting, some little beck he had

found for himself, and the old man that lives down there, Mick Cullen, no relation, found him struggling and gasping on the grass. He was nigh blue in the face from lack of breath, but he was still awake, and he was pointing fiercely with a finger at his throat. Mick opened his mouth like he would be looking at a horse's teeth, and saw there was a mess of bread and cheese down there. He thrust in his no doubt grimy hand and foostered about and his fingers touched on something small and hard, and he gripped it, and pulled it out. This gave breath to Matt, but the little item ripped the inside of his throat as it came out, for it proved to be a long thorn, that had lodged sideways there, in Matt's throat. So then there was blood and pain, and Mick stopped the new van on the road that brings the new bakery bread to Kiltegan, heaven help us, and Matt was fetched into Baltinglass. His throat was swelling all the time, because the thorn off of a tree is a bad thorn, it will have rubbish on the tip. Mick was thinking he might have to punch a hole in Matt's neck. But he's in a bed in the hospital. And they think he will be all right in a few days. He's breathing like a sick bullock, says Mick. And he is lucky to be alive.'

'I was down that way and saw nothing.'

'Well, that's it. He could have just died where he was. I only just heard the story from one of the O'Toole boys that was coming up by the forest track. They know we know him.'

'I will go down to Baltinglass and see him, Sarah. You must mind the children. Egg in a cup they want for tea.'

'All right, Annie. If you go down now you will hardly be back tonight. Maybe they will give you a niche in the hospital.'

'It is not a place I want to spend the night.'

'Why so, Annie?'

'They can call it what they like, but it is still the old county home where my poor father breathed his last.'

'God rest him. Don't mind that old story now, Annie. Matt needs someone by him.'

'All right, Sarah.'

'Bring your old nightgown, just in case.'

'I will.'

'And a change of knickers.'

'I will.'

'You don't want them to be thinking we don't change our underclothes.'

'We don't.'

Then she goes to the half-door and leans out, roaring.

'Come in, come in, children, come in, come in!' Then turns to me again. 'I am missing Red Dandy,' she says. 'I can spot her nowhere.'

'She'll be hiding in the barn,' I say. 'That is her wont.'

'Aye. She will come to the grain tonight, I'm sure.'

I pack my few things in a bundle and I kiss the returning children, and go.

'Annie,' says the little boy, 'Annie, come here a minute, will you?'

'I can't now,' I say, my feet already set for the Baltinglass road, passing on, passing on.

He comes down to the old round pillars of the gates. The moss grows lightly there, and little ferns. Sometimes I lean there, in less fervent days, watching the failing of the light, stroking the smooth old stones. It is the mark of the place, those pillars, pillars almost of dreams.

'I want to be whispering secrets,' he says, in the very language of Wicklow. His Dublin ways are deserting him. It is not just the butter that is in him now, but even the words of Kelsha. *I want to be whispering secrets . . .*

'And we will whisper all our secrets, when I get back,' I say. I won't worry him with the reason for my going. He is a worrier, a worrier, like my own father. 'Don't worry yourself. Bye-bye.'

'Bye-bye, Auntie Anne.' He lifts a hand, like a country boy. 'Bye-bye!'

'We thought it was a fishbone,' says the little nurse, dressed in her suit as tightly as a rosebud, all round, pink flesh and white starch, 'but he was not eating fish. We carefully examined it, and deemed it to be a thorn, of a hawthorn maybe. He was only eating bread and cheese. So it is a mystery.'

I nod my head. I am beginning to be very uncomfortable about this talk of thorns. I have gained a lift, and was dropped off at the old grey gates of the county — of the hospital. There is little change. The same sad laurels line the avenue. The low, one-storey building still lies in the grass like a fallen cross. I think of that bleak day, turning in here in the Ford, my father clear raving in the back, then dragged into the heavy precincts of the home, and then placed in a lone, locked room. I will never forget his silence then, his hunched figure in his ill-fitting suit — for he was shrinking away with age — the entire defeat of the man. He knew where he was and did not know why I was putting him there. He could not see his own violence, his own rage, it was invisible to him. He could not fathom why a daughter would bury her father there, in that deep, dark room.

'I will go and see him, if I may,' I say, just like in days of old, when I would visit my degraded father.

'You may,' she says. 'Oh, he is breathing much better. His throat inside is hard and sore, and will be horrible uncomfortable for him now the while. But he will mend, we do hope.'

'You are sure and certain?' I say.

'You are what to him, ma'am?' she says, and sadly, sadly, yes, she glances at my bowed back. 'Sister, wife?'

'Not wife, God forbid. I am a maiden woman. I am his sister-in-law. But, we are close-knit.'

Why do I say God forbid, when in truth . . . No matter. She is only looking for information, she is writing it down now on a card, *sister-in-law* . . .

'And his true wife, where is she?'

What does that mean, true wife?

'She is dead, Nurse, she is no more.'

'And what was her name?'

'Maud, it was.'

'And your own?'

'It is Annie Dunne.'

'And his nearest relative would be then?'

'His son, Tim, but he is in Spain. Then there is his son Trevor, but he is in England. He has brothers, but some of them are dead, and he has a . . . he does not go home to Cork where he comes from, I don't know why . . .'

'Oh, well,' she says, brightly, quite fed up with such complications. 'Well, so, you must do as next of kin, if we had to, you know, operate, or the like.'

'I think I would do.'

'Well, sure his eyes are open. He is not unconscious. Go in and have a gander, Annie.'

'Thank you, I will.'

And off goes her small person, her scrunched-up buttocks heaving about in the uniform as she disappears into the ancient shadows of the corridor. It was in the last room, behind the last door, that my father lay. In that time there was a ward close by with the madwomen of the district strapped to the beds, and when my father cried out in the nights with mournful horrors, he would set off the great long rows of grandmothers and mothers and aunts, wailing and caterwauling. It was a terrible, accusing sound, the sound of our refuse, as one might say, and our failure of love. His solo sorrow, their dark choir of pain. Now such unwanted women are in the new mental asylum in Carlow, still in their rows, but the beds and walls are new. God keep Sarah and me from such drastic fates.

I peep into Matt's quarters. It is a shock to see him. His face is blotchy and streaked. They have not washed the mud off him, which may well be the mere mud attaching in a usual, daily fashion to Mick Cullen, who is after all, a digger of drains. Which is why Sarah Cullen always says, *no relation.*

I think it is that even the sunlight here is old, comes from another time through the exhausted windows. It lies anyhow at the foot of Matt's bed. He looks like a saint of old, some hardy creature washed up there, a worn-out boxer or the like, perhaps a victorious boxer half destroyed by his own victory. Well, he looks resplendent enough. His eyes are indeed open, but he holds his head still, he sees me there but does not move that head. Even from the door I can see the swollen neck. It is angry and red. But a blackthorn is a bad thorn, as anyone knows, when it sticks in a person's hand it lends a severe ache long after it is pulled out.

How do I know it was a blackthorn? Well I know it. He was eating his bread and cheese.

I approach his bed, contrite and smiling. He tries to give a small nod of greeting, but immediately his eyes scrunch up with pain.

'Don't move yourself, Matt,' I say, 'don't trouble yourself. I am sorry to see you like this. The nurse says you will quickly mend.'

But of course he cannot reply. There is an unworthy feeling in me now, a kind of petty triumph. I could do him harm now. I could dispatch him from life in this weakened state. Of course I do not want to, he is too dear to me, to the children, to the memory of Maud. But and, I could. That is the point.

But I cast that thought from my mind. I must not think thoughts in that manner. And why ever do I think such thoughts? I am already responsible, though I hope innocently, for his present predicament.

It will have been my butter he brought for his sandwich, the wrap of butter I gave him in friendship, with the thorn off a blackthorn tree in it, to keep it fresh.

Did I tell him there would be a thorn in the butter? I do not think so, and him in truth a city man, and so not expecting such an item.

God forgive me, he may think I was trying to murder him, if ever he finds out.

Into my mind, I know not why, swims the picture of Cupid with his bow. But the thorn of a blackthorn bush is a poor dart for such a purpose.

Maybe I meant to kill him. Maybe there is a darkness in me, that meant to do him harm, without me even knowing. I shiver in this possibility of evil, I shiver. The more I think it, the more true I feel it. Guilt grips me, guilt grips me, and then suddenly I laugh, laugh at myself and my terrible notions. I have no wish to kill Matt. And he will not know about butter and thorns. It will remain a mystery, it will, mercifully.

Oh, I am laughing like a hag at his bedside. His eyes open wider, questioning maybe. But I have no answers to his questions, no grist for his mill, for the mills of the world grind everything exceedingly small and rough. No verse for his chapter, no path for his woods.

They put me that night into my father's old room. It is a strange coincidence. No other room can take me, and otherwise I would be sitting on a hard chair in the corridor. I tell myself it will be no worse than spending a night at Lathaleer, that a living person must not fear the dead, especially if the dead was close and precious to her heart.

And I sleep a clear and restful night. I wonder at the accident that has brought me there. For what purpose? Such peace, such rest. No dreams, no frighting thoughts. It is very strange. Though I fear the room greatly as I enter, they have painted the old yellow walls with a fresh, buttery colour, there are a few coals burning in the once famished grate, and the iron bed that was his raft of dreams is gone, replaced by a spanking new thing of shining chrome. The sheets, which in his day were speckled by mildews and filth, are Belfast quality and well starched. The atmosphere of the room has been allayed, removed. It is just a place, a new place. His ghost is gone.

And yet in another way I feel his ghost, benign and loving, fatherly and kind. I have lain on the bed and looked at the ceiling that he looked at, in the watches of his last days. And there is no terror. I think it is that he has wrapped me round all that night. His released soul watches over me, his ageing daughter. In that place where I thought I witnessed only horror, perhaps I was in some manner mistaken. Maybe it was not horror I was looking at, all those years ago, twenty-five years and more, a man stripped of all uniforms and honours, duties and family, even kings and country. Maybe the horror was only in me, as I gazed on my fallen father. For his ghost, if ghost it is that lets me sleep, sleep finer than for many a year, is benign and calm.

Maybe now I think it was not horror after all that I was looking at, in those fled days, but courage.

I wake in the morning, feeling clear, clearer than for many a year. The day itself is clear, fresh and bright. The old building in its dress of stones is already warm, taking its general temperature from the summer, like the sea. All is silence, dustlessness and neatness. The little nurse is back on duty, prim and peachy. Matt's throat has subsided in the small hours, giving him respite. The look of worry has gone from the nurse, the look of pain has gone from Matt.

'We will let him home by evening time tomorrow,' says the little nurse. It is an aftermath. Peaceful birdsong on the battle-field.

I want to tell Matt about Billy Kerr, but I do not think his condition allows it. I know he would be scandalized by such intentions. He is a highly moral man. He would go and take Billy Kerr by the scruff of the neck, and . . . But then they are friends, so perhaps I should not be so sure. I am sure and certain of very little, truth to tell. I want to recruit Matt to my cause, but suddenly there is doubt in me that he would readily enlist. He is recently married for the second time himself, a thing some Catholic widowers will not do, though he has chosen in his Anna a woman the same age as himself. There he is a-bed, the twice-married man. But where are his wives now? Who has cared for him? Ah, yes.

'I will get Billy Kerr to fetch you to-morrow, if you like,' I say, lamely enough.

'That will be grand,' he says.

That day I spend idle in the gardens of the hospital, now and then returning in to check on Matt. Then I sense in myself that secret clock that says, this is long enough to leave Sarah with the children. They will have worn her out.

Matt, with rasping voice, thanks me for my night vigil. Little does he know how deep I slept, how watchless I was. And so I shake his hand, and thumb a lift for Kelsha.

In the old days, a passing cart could not easily decline to give your bum a perch. Cars sail by without a nod or wave, strangers from Carlow town maybe, from Dublin, Wicklow. There is a dejection in such matters, but I do not feel it. I am buoyant, almost, I am thinking, graceful, or at least, full of a kind of grace, bestowed upon me. High clouds rage in the upper sky, they rage with sunlight pouring down through them in yellow torrents. There may be a change in the weather coming. I know what I look like to the passing cars, an old countrywoman without trap or new-fangled vehicle to her name, but I do not care. I know my worth. Yes, my father was chief superintendent of the Dublin Metropolitan Police, B Division, with responsibility for the Castle herself. But those days are gone, that world is no more, it did not even have a requiem. My cousin is the Bishop of Nara, but, God help those wild Africans, he does not care even for me, and would not help me in my hour of need. So let it be, as things are. I am a simple woman that shares a berth with Sarah Cullen. I work from dawn till dusk for my food and lodging. Soon I may again be homeless, hearthless, adrift. Perhaps I will be like an old woman of the roads, in the upshot, damp and wandering, with the real stars for a coverlet. Perhaps that will be my battle, what God ordains. I do not know. I am a solitary nothing, and on this morning of the world, by a ditch at the edge of Baltinglass, waiting for a friendly car, I am wonderfully happy.

I reach the farm by nightfall. The children I imagine are long a-bed. That bucket I notice is still where it was, out of place, upturned. The yard is all shadows, secretive, hiding itself in bundles and fardels of darkness. It is strange to be out so late, to come in from the countryside like a traveller, to a place so known, so loved.

Sarah is hungry for the news. I tell her all, without restraint.

'That is very good, Annie,' she says. 'You have done well. And look at you, with that shining countenance. You don't look a day over twenty.'

She is very relieved, and laughing now at her own wit.

'Not a day,' she says, firmly, as if I might

disagree. But I am so tired now I am almost sleeping in the chair.

'Come on,' she says, 'and get yourself to bed. A night in an unfamiliar room is exhausting to the spirit.'

'I knew the room,' I say.

'Oh?'

'No, it is the worry, and the walking has tired me out. I am happy enough to be tired. I will sleep tonight.'

'It is a comfort certainly, the land of dreams.'

'It is, Sarah, it is.'

Again I sleep the sleep of the blessed.

Chapter Fifteen

But the next day there is something nagging at the back of my mind. It is washday, so we suffer the deluge of linen and water, we scrape, we scrub, we wring, we wrestle, our arms are reddened by the waters and the soaps, scoured by the bleach. There is a beautiful drying wind blowing, we are eager to get the sheets and shifts on the drying-bushes as early as we can. By mid-afternoon we have all accomplished. Our range of bushes looks like a fleet under full sail, with little quiet cracks in the playful breezes. But that unknown something is on the tip of my tongue. The calendar in the corner of the kitchen, that Mrs Nicodemus gives us at Christmastide, says the fifth of July, but that rings no bell. I am beginning to be tormented by it.

The little girl and boy keep asking me to play with them. I am run ragged by their requests. Sometimes the adult soul cannot put itself to childish things. So for the most part of the day they are wandering about the yard. They play some game they have invented with pebbles, then they sit by the forgotten stones and tell each other elaborate stories. I notice that they are giving me now and then strange little looks, almost glowering looks. I do not understand them this day.

Sarah and myself are in the kitchen, sucking gratefully on cups of tea. I am already looking forward to bed, if I am always to sleep in this new manner, as fresh as a babe. What a weariness there is, what a drain of blood from the limbs.

'I am so pleased Matt weathered his difficulty,' says Sarah, suddenly, just I suppose because the thought rose in her head, made a ring of water there like the nose of a trout.

'Matt!' I say. 'Oh, blessed Matt. All day I have been . . . I said I would get Billy Kerr to go down for him. Oh, mercy . . .'

I rouse myself. This is a foolish lapse. I do not even know if Billy Kerr will be down at the Dunnes, and Matt, I am sure, will be waiting as patient as a dog for him, and as trusting as a dog in my power of arrangements. I am vexed with myself, and fussed.

'I will go down and tell him,' I say.

'Oh, Annie, after all the work we've been put to,' says Sarah.

'I must, I must.'

When I go out again, the change in the weather that yesterday seemed to predict has taken hold of the sky and the trees. The little boy is over at that upturned bucket. He has a hand under the rim and is looking in. When he sees me looking, he drops the bucket guiltily, and stands up straight, and looks at me with a startled face. I turn my head back in the door.

'You had better take the washing in, Sarah,' I say. 'There seems to be a bit of rain brewing.'

'All right, Annie. Sure they'll be bone-dry anyhow.'

'They will not, but, what can you do?'

The little boy has skithered away into the barn. I go over to the zinc bucket and lift it myself. Cowled with darkness inside stands Red Dandy, looking very woebegone for herself. Her little head rocks from side to side, her eyes seem to be spinning in their reddened sockets. She looks like a man that has been drinking for three days, or should I say, a ballet dancer, what with her rumpled tutu. I lift the bucket off completely.

'What ails you, Red Dandy?' I say. 'Has that child done something to you?'

Then I do remember seeing the bucket in this position yesterday. How long has this poor hen been penned within? One day, two days? Without food, without light. Now she tries to walk across the yard to where the cock is strutting indifferently. He doesn't care what horrors befall his wives. She keeps falling down and getting up, and pecks at the ground in a way that suggests her wits are addled. Hunger and darkness have undone her quite.

Now I am not only fussed, but I am fixed by an unaccustomed rage. I am fierce to go and find the boy and accuse him, but first I must find him. Red Dandy is — could I call her my dowry, part of my dowry, that I brought to Sarah when I came so I would not come with nothing? The little boy must understand what he has done. Oh, another little voice says, calm yourself, Annie, calm and ease, calm and ease, but I do not heed it.

The little boy is cowering in the barn. I have never seen him cower before. It is as sure a proof of guilt as I could ask for. God forgive me, but I pull him to me by the arm, and give his backside a firm slap. I slap it again, and then once more. He wriggles in my grasp, but the second time he does not move at all, he stands quite still, and my hand hits his backside without resistance. He stares at me with his brown eyes. I have never hit him before in my life. Suddenly it is like a dream, a nightmare. I am so horrified at myself that my anger redoubles and kindles and flares. I am thinking, but he deserves it. He has been ugly and filthy with his sister! Licking, licking, and kneeling! I am afraid now I will kill him, so I step back and raise myself above him impressively.

'Why did you do that, you horrible little boy? Why did you do that?'

'I didn't!' he says.

Now his sister appears from nowhere, the nowhere that children spend so much of their day in, forgotten by the grown-ups and unseen.

'Don't hit that boy!' she says.

'You be quiet now, girl, or you'll get the same. He has put the bucket on Red Dandy and she is mad in the head now from that ordeal. How could you torture a creature so? You are evil and cruel! You are doing things with your sister that no one in the world could understand! You are disgusting!'

Even in my rage I am thinking, what are you saying, what are you saying?

'I am not! I did not! I did not put the bucket on Red Dandy! I found him under the bucket!'

'You did not find him under the bucket! You put her there!'

'I did not! I thought he lived there!'

'First the fire engine, and now the hen!'

'You put my new fire engine in the filthy muck, Auntie Anne. I hate you, I hate you!'

'So, you hate me!' And I grab his arm again. 'So, you hate me!' Hot scalding tears pour down my face, his face is dry and red. 'So you talk about oranges in secret and you hate me! It is horrible, all horrible. It is not like children and childhood! Where is your innocence, oh, where is your innocence?' The little girl is pulling on my polka-dot apron.

'Stop,' she says, 'stop! You're like Daddy, you're like Daddy. Stop, stop!'

'Daddy will eat you!' cries the boy.

'You put the bucket on Red Dandy, didn't you, because I put the fire engine in the dunghill! Oh, and I thought you had been generous about it, but you were easy and going about happy-seeming, because you had taken your revenge! You had done something bad, bad! Isn't that it? Isn't that it? I will beat you! I will beat you till you tell me!'

But the little girl takes action then, she kicks me on the shins with all her strength. It is astonishingly sore. I drop the little

298

boy's arm. He races away along the lane between the barn and the horse byre.

'I have no time to deal with this now,' I shout after him. 'And your poor grandfather in the hospital!'

So I flounce myself out of the yard and down the track. For as long as I can I try to preserve my anger, because behind the anger there is something much worse than it — the knowledge of what I have done. The children are in my care, and I have let the exhaustion of the work, of Matt, of the whole summer of Billy Kerr's intrigues, loose me from my habitual nature, and become for those moments a mere savage heart. Even under the wall of O'Toole's farm, I am deep in remorse. Oh, I will make it up to them now when I return. I will go into Mrs Nicodemus and buy some mighty sweets. I will, I will. God allow them to forgive me.

I find Billy Kerr among the outhouses of Feddin.

'Can you go in and fetch Matt?' I say, 'From the hospital. He will be expecting you.'

'Why will he be expecting me?'

'Because I said you would collect him this evening.'

'It is nearly evening now, Annie. You didn't think to tell me before this?'

'I am telling you now!'

'You are, Annie, and but that it is Matt, poor Matt now that has had a fright, I would think twice now about harnessing the sisters' pony and going all the way without friendly notice to Baltinglass.'

'Will you fetch him, or will you not fetch him?'

'I will fetch him.'

'Good,' I say, and turn about-heel, and away.

When I get to the village, I find the shop of Mrs Nicodemus. I peer in the sparkling window. I can see her counting money, and marking her books at the counter. I tap on the glass. She looks up and sees me. She shakes her head.

When I get back up the green road to Kelsha, there is worse to befall me. I find Sarah and the little girl scouring the offices of the yard, as if they might be in a strange frenzy of finding eggs. They are kneeling and peering under things, and pulling loose boards, and calling the boy's name.

'What is it, Sarah, now, what is it?'

'Look at it growing dark,' she says, 'and

the child is missing. The child is missing, Annie.'

'How could a child be missing in all the simple spaces of these acres. It is not possible.'

'He knows how to hide himself,' says the girl. 'He is an expert.'

'And do you know where he is, girl?' I say, with that touch of anger I fear myself.

'She doesn't, Annie,' says Sarah. 'We have been searching now all the time you were gone.'

'He ran away out through the lane there, and into the field,' I say. 'Did you search the sloping field?'

'We were all around it. The girl helped me. She said you were angry with him, Annie. Why were you angry?'

'Because he put the bucket on Red Dandy!'

'He did not,' says the girl.

'Well, somebody did,' I say, 'and he had good reason.'

'He didn't,' says the girl. 'And now you've gone and lost him. Don't you know what day it is, Auntie Anne?'

'No, what day is it?' I say, and then I remember. It was not Matt's lift was nagging at my mind after all, but this other fact, that now the little girl offers me. But

I know it already.

'It is his birthday,' she says. 'And he got no present. And he made me say nothing, because of the fire engine. He is mighty sorry about the fire engine. That's how he is. He's not the boy to put buckets on hens. He thinks you will never forgive him. He's having bad dreams. Last night he said he wanted to die!'

'Don't say that, I can't hear it!' I cry. 'Wanted to die! And no sign of him now. Is God going to punish me thus? Am I to be riven and harrowed by sorrow?'

'Calm yourself, Annie,' says Sarah. 'Go in to Mary Callan and ask if she has seen him.'

'Maybe she has taken him!'

'Why would she do that?'

'A strange old woman that lives in filth!'

'Annie, be calm. We must be calm.'

'Maybe Billy Kerr has stolen him, like he said he would.'

'Billy Kerr? Annie! Haven't you just seen him?'

'My fear is, Sarah,' I say, 'and I do not want to come across you and your plans, is that — is that Billy Kerr has taken him.'

'Sure, why in all the world would he be doing such a thing?'

'You don't how he has been persecuting

me! I fear it, I fear it!'

'Annie, Annie, go in to Nanny Callan and ask. Billy Kerr took no one. I do not know why you say he did.'

I know I am gabbling. But it is hard to describe the horror that sits in me, the fright, the misery. My stomach is being dragged wholesale from its pit. For some wild reason, the old practices of the Inquisition, that seemed to preoccupy now and then my father's thoughts, flood into my head. For it is what it feels like — a secret frame of wood, my limbs stretched tight upon it. I cannot endure this absence of the little boy. I feel like running wildly about, tearing through hedgerows, flying over hills and ploughland, crying great cries, if I could only lay eyes on him again. And I know it has been the violence of my own hands that has driven him from me. He was in my care and I have sundered him from that care, caused him to tear himself from the refuge of Kelsha. By my own actions! Would I not do anything now, climb any crag, level any wall or prison, just to discover him warm and well, and gather him into my arms?

I veritably leap the road and climb the rough wall into Mary Callan's precincts. I have never been near her hovel before, but only passed it with the curse of my eye. I approach the little patch of flagstones at her door and start to call her name. She comes immediately to the half-door. She does not speak.

'Mary Callan,' I say, 'have you seen my child? I mean, my sister's son's child. He has run away from us.'

She does not speak. She is silent. She pushes open her door and stands in the morsel of yard.

'Can you not speak to me, woman, and tell me, you wretched crone!'

She only looks at me. Is she thinking, or is there a vacancy of mind entire and complete?

I put a hand on her bony shoulder and almost shake it.

'Will you not tell me? Did you see that little boy? Woman, woman, did you see him?'

She shakes off my hand with a simple gesture, like a pony does, a shying away of sorts. She goes away down her path like a hedgehog, and out her broken gate and onto the green road, never looking back. I must have frightened her out of her skin.

'Will you not help me?' I call.

When I reach the yard again — I can see

Sarah and the little girl searching the ditch of the sloping field — and cross the inert shape of Shep in the yard, murdered as usual with exhaustion, you might think, on an inspiration gleaned from some forgotten book, I go back into the house and fetch out from his bedroom a gansey of the boy. When I see his empty bed, his small collection of diminutive clothes, his shorts, his shoes, his socks, I burst into tears. But I take myself from tears, savagely, and I bring the gansey out to Shep and shove it under his uninterested nose. All he does is rise shakily on his spindly legs, like an animal truly well past his time for shooting, and there is a part of me in this extreme that would get some relief from shooting him, and then he wanders in sleepily to the barn, and then out he comes again, without a murmur let alone a bark of enthusiasm, and settles himself once more in front of me on the still-warm stones.

Should I be going down to Kiltegan to fetch the sergeant? It would take so long. And is the sergeant in his fits of despair? There has been no sign of him about the place for weeks. I do not know his condition. Would Mrs Nicodemus help me? But why do I think of her? It is because she has lost a child, she will know this ripping in the chest, this plunging of despair. Who is there to help me, outside Sarah? Matt will be waiting in Baltinglass, even Billy Kerr I have dispatched to get him. There is no one. My head is wild. I have never felt the like. Oh, in the old fled days you could raise the district. Now there is no district, only a cruel sequence of separate lives, in a sad line of worthless pearls all down to the main road. Alone in our anguish!

Then a black thought takes hold of me, thinking on these inhabitants around me. Jack Furlong! The rabbit man! The rabbit man with his murderous song, his murdered mother, his mad brother! Maybe the poor child has wandered as far as him, and some terrible fate has . . . No, no, Jack Furlong is a gentle man enough. But maybe he has wandered up there, by the snaking path, maybe . . . Maybe he is following that old story I told him, about his grandfather and the dog, in the woods, in the woods . . . Oh, no whirlpool at the bottom of a falls could be so embroiled in circles and currents. I will go mad now if I do not mind — if I do not find that boy.

I shout to Sarah, 'I am going up the hill!' and she straightens from her search and nods. There is a growing darkness now in things: the sheaves of shadows heap themselves into the bread-and-butter bushes, the whin bushes at the top of the sloping field look like calves lying down before the night.

Into the woods I go, the scrubby pines, the stunted ash trees. I am thinking of my father as a little boy, bringing the condemned dog into trees like these, determined, alarmed, distraught. How strange, intent are these boys of ours. How resolute, how brave! But he will not like this scumbling twilight, if he has entered here. No child could, and he does not have a dog for companion. Why I think he might be following an old story I do not know, it is just a thought, an inspiration. Soon I believe it must be so, soon I believe somewhere in these woods, in some darkening glade, I will discover him. I call and call his name.

I rise up further through the trees, feeling the roof of Kelsha dropping below, sensing the leaving behind of civilized things, of lights, of fires, of rooms. Now I am in the realm of the rabbits, the harvest of Jack Furlong. I am suddenly encouraged by this thought, because I tell myself, of course, Jack Furlong knows every farthing of these woods, every path, every fallen tree to make a sheltering cave. He will find the child in a trice. Of course, of course! How foolish I have been. There is help at hand after all!

I come out onto the ridge of that small world and see the single light of Jack Furlong's cottage on the further ridge. How wild and cold it is here in winter, now it is like a summer meadow of old, when lands such as these were held in common, and people spent all the summer months on these pastures with their cows. I stumble across hillock and stumps and bang on his rain-stripped door.

There is no answer. What am I to do? I open his door and look in, hoping he might be asleep in his chair. It is a bleak sight that meets my eyes. The room looks like it was not cleaned for years, most likely since the day his mother was killed. There is a chair by the filthy fire, and all about it lie layers and layers of paper and discarded things. There are mildewed cups and plates, old relics of real lives, there are mounds of peelings, of cabbages, potatoes, God knows what. It is like the nest of a rat. The only clean thing is the rows upon rows of rabbit skins, all neatly hanging on long strings, like a crazy ceiling of fur. There is the stench as of death throughout the room. And this is where a man lives, a man who emerges from here to walk the hills with a clean aspect enough, and trim clothes enough. A miracle. But there is no Jack Furlong in this nest.

'Child, child!' I call. 'Wherever are you?'

There is no answer, only the well-known soughing of the wind. That freshening weather is everywhere now, the smaller branches lash about gently, there are gusts and whimpers in the woods. It is cold now, cold. I pull my cardigan about me tightly. I feel like a creature that has been disembowelled, and must carry on regardless, to escape this horror of a hand that seeks to crush me.

Oh, it has grown so dark. I can barely mark the path by which I climbed. I hurry back down, terrified now I might lose my way myself, and be no earthly use to the boy. My greater terror is that he might be taken, that those tinkers themselves marauding as they do might have secreted him away. That he might be bound tight on a cart somewhere, anywhere among the roads, and be going, pace by pace, away from me, never to be found again. I have heard of such tragedies! And his father and mother in London, knowing nothing of my carelessness, my crime. As yet, as yet! I will be castigated, condemned, imprisoned, and all of that I will welcome if he is not found. Oh, I must not think these thoughts, I must calm in some fashion, or I will die.

I come down onto the sloping field. I do not know how long I have been gone, maybe an hour. The field is bare. I cannot see light in the house because the gable below me is blind of windows. But I do see figures coming up the green road, bearing torches. It is like a picture from some other time, some other century. The flames leap from the torches like the fiery hair of tinkers. Is it the tinkers themselves? I am sore confused. Oh, my legs have no ounce of strength to carry me, but I force them on. Will man or God ever forgive me? I do not care. Let there be news to soothe my soul!

I come down into the yard. The figures have reached the round columns of the gates and flood forward to meet me. It is hard to see the faces in the whirling light, the little storm now engaging strongly with the flames. But I hear the voice of Billy Kerr. There is a woman beside him. And another woman. And three or four men I cannot say I know. And children too, responsible ages of children. And Sarah stands there, tightly holding the hand of the little girl, whose face I notice is as white as the moon's, riding now in the arms of the sycamores.

'Any news, Sarah, any news?'

'No, Annie, dear — you?'

'I was all up by Jack Furlong's and the common woods. No sign, no sign. What are we to do?'

'We will search for him,' says a voice. It is Billy Kerr. 'The whole district is raised and we will find him. We will search everywhere and everything till we have him found and safe.'

For it is Billy Kerr with the leading torch. And that is Mary Callan at his side, heaving with a lack of breath. And there surely is Mrs Nicodemus. And those faces are the faces of men I see as I pass, but do not greet, labourers of the O'Tooles and the more stately O'Tooles themselves.

'Mary Callan came down with news of your distress,' says Billy Kerr. 'I lit the torches and came straight up.'

So there is a district. It is myself that has no district, no sense of it, but it is there despite me. Then I remember, staring at her, a thing it is only stupidity to forget. Mary Callan cannot speak. I have a hump and she has a crookedness in the throat, two things to keep a woman on her own. She has no voice, no way to tell a thing. She has gone

311

down to her cousin to fetch us help.

All this a torrent of thinking. There is no lightning in this mild summer storm, but nevertheless lights are leaping in my eyes, not just the torches. I realize I am close to fainting. I feel it all down my legs, and in my cheeks.

'First we will search the further road,' says Billy Kerr. 'We'll go on up, lads!' he calls, and the *meitheal* of people surges forward. I have dark visions now of ponds and rivers, of the twists of hay with candles on them set upon the water, to find out anything snagged beneath the surface. It is dark and I am weeping. I will never see the boy again. There is no other way to think it. He is gone, he is dead.

I look up the yard, something draws my eye. The bulk of the trap looms in the harrowing lines of new darkness. But another element is there also, a thin white shadow at the murky rim of the trap. Shep is veritably cavorting now. He rushes into the barn as if to declare, see, see I showed you all this before, you didn't believe me, old human woman of little faith. It is the boy, it is surely the boy. My head is all muddle and miracle in one stew.

'Billy Kerr, Billy Kerr!' I cry. 'Come back, come back!'

I am afraid I am merely seeing things. I need the proof of other eyes. But I am sure, truly. Unless it is an angel in the trap, a vision.

Now Billy Kerr comes back from the pitch-dark of the mountain road, his torch making the small landscape jump about. I can see his balding pate shining under the freckling starlight. Such a night of stars is ahead of us! Mary Callan, wizened and small, trots after him, moving as surely and black as a boatman in the water bucket, renewed, feeling I am sure the same bolts of energy that I do myself, reinvigorating old legs.

'He's found,' I say, 'he's found! Oh, child, child.'

And forward up the yard I go, feeling my legs as heavy as oak beams after all the scuttering and scattering about, and I sweep to the back of the trap where the little wooden door hangs open, and I hold my hands aloft to him. Without another word he descends into my arms, loosing himself from his intent like an apple from the glue of its twig, twisting down into my arms from his childish madness. What a small length of bones he is, so warm and nice his back, the little slope of the shoulders, the funny, rough, sudden legs of him.

He nestles into my old breast, moulding himself there like plasticine. I hug him and hug him.

'Oh, child, child,' I say. 'You were lost and now you are found. I am glad, I am glad!'

Suddenly there is that wiggling that children do when they want to be released. I do not understand. We are hardly wed again, and yet that is the way of children. He has seen someone else coming up behind me, because I hear Matt's voice.

'My God, I heard the boy was lost! I heard from the girls of Lathaleer that my little man was lost!'

'Papa, Papa,' he cries, like a very Biblical child indeed, 'I was hiding but Annie has found me!'

I turn about. I see the little boy going up into Matt's arms. I feel a thousand things and nothing at all. The human part of me feels such great relief, such love, such gratitude to God to have returned this child safely to us, for all the reasons his safety is essential, to me, to his parents, to Matt, to Sarah, the little girl, maybe even to God himself. The ugly part of me, the creaturely, feels dejected and cheated, robbed, imprisoned, despairing. I cannot explain it, it is like a weapon, a rope of water falling from the hills. All a great muddle of things, and at the midst of this muddle swirls something without a name, something dark, ferocious, starless. Matt stares into my eyes, luxuriating in the poultice, the bower, the harbour of the little boy.

'Magritte!' I say, I know not why.

It is all I can say, before our yard in Kelsha begins to turn and turn like a great mill-pool, and then there is a roaring as of the sea at Silver Strand by the bay of Wicklow, and then there is peculiar silence, and then there is blackness.

There is a most peculiar stench, and then a thought of knitting, pearl and plain, pearl and plain, endless and endless, peculiar, unbidden, and then the faces round me, Sarah and Matt, and the more stray moon of Billy Kerr.

'Poor Annie. Are you all right, dear?' says Sarah.

'Oh, oh — I am fine,' I say. I feel like the peas gone to mush in the pot.

'You were very clever, Annie,' says Matt. 'To find the boy. How did you find him, how did you find him?'

'I didn't,' I say. 'He found himself.'

And there is a pause. 'He found himself!'

I say again, my fogs and miseries entirely lifting, old rooks from the ground, to their nests, nesting, nesting, and they are beginning to laugh. And I am laughing.

'He found himself!' says Matt, and there is that strange, rare screeching of laughter that people do when great strains are taken off them, and they can breathe again, as ordinary human beings, beyond emergency.

'He found himself!' says Sarah, bending as lithe as a willow, no sign of the yard brush that her back usually is.

'He found himself!' I echo. 'He found himself, he found himself!'

I fold the little girl and boy into their beds, harbour them there like little boats, wedge them in with blankets and pillows. I am nesting them truly.

'What a wild little boy he is,' says the girl, 'to be hiding and causing all that to-do.'

She does not seem to resent me now. She is smiling. There is a grace in her, an understanding maybe. I do not know whether to upbraid her for kicking my shin. She was protecting her brother, it was a good thing she did. Let it go by, let it all go by, with the help of God. My own violence with it, I pray, the stain of my own violence. I pray to God. Let there be no damage beyond repair, no perfect things in smithereens. Please God, I pray.

'He is, I suppose, a wild little boy enough.' The solace of banter! 'But, his feelings were sore hurt. Weren't they?'

'They were,' he says, a mite glumly. The rainbows of excitement have abated. What is left is the mud and murmur after the storm. It is a very strange spot to be, I remember well from my own young days. I feel sorry for him. I take his little sack of bones again in my bony arms, and hold him against me as gently as I can.

'Do you miss your mother?' I say, on an inspiration.

'No,' he says. 'I miss you, Auntie Anne.'

'But, child, I am here.'

'Is it ever going to be the same, like it was at the start?' he says.

'Nothing is ever the same as at the start. It changes, and then it is different, but it is good different oftentimes.'

'But you will not be forgiving me, Auntie Anne.'

I am breathing into his face, an oval of heat and simplicity.

'I will be forgiving you with all my heart, without reservation. I was forgiving you

317

the moment I saw you in the trap. You are already forgiven. And I hope you will forgive me.'

'I did not go putting the bucket on Red Dandy,' he says. 'I did not.'

'It's no odds if you put it on her or did not. It is not the important thing, a bit of a hen. It is you is the important thing. I have you home now in your bed, that is the important thing.'

'I would like to tell you, I didn't put the bucket on him.'

'On her. And now if you say you did not, I will believe you.'

'You did not believe me before, which is why I hid.'

'Now I believe you.'

And I kiss him.

Sarah comes in with a little bowl. In it is an unguent she has crushed for him. I think it is of boiled nettles and hogweed, which she keeps in a pot for her rheumatism. She lifts his sheet, and opens his pyjamas and marks it in a line down the line of breastbone.

'What is that for, Sarah?' I whisper.

'It is to let him sleep with good dreams after his ordeal. It will heal him.'

How strange she is, I suppose. She does not speak directly to the child, and yet the child trusts her. She does not kiss him, nor have one word for him. Now that I think of it, she never truly speaks to them. She does not tuck them in. And yet no woman ever laid a finger so gentle on that breastbone, nor spoke of dreams and healing with so soft a voice. I wish I could learn what it is that she is, what a receptacle of simple manners she is. She is just there, like a creature, or like a god, neither of which use words. Other means, deeper, older, darker. And true, when she goes out again, there is a change in the boy. He is the boy he was. Even I feel now hopeful and at ease, no matter what comes. Is there not eternal pleasure and peace in the facts of human love, that overrides present difficulties? I do think so.

'I am sorry for the green fire engine. I am sorry for fetching it out of its hiding place in the barn, and trodding on it. It was just a game, a good game I found to do.'

'It was your birthday present. It was yours to do with as you liked.'

'I should have waited for the day. I should have.'

'But this *is* the day. This is your birthday. And tomorrow we will go down to Baltinglass together, and you will have the choice of the shop there. That is my promise.'

Now big, difficult boyhood tears tear from him. He is heaving painfully, his breath robbed each time he cries out, then a gap, a silence, and the hot, ferocious tears. His chest shakes with the effort to cry, to breathe. The ice is loosed on the little hill of himself, and now down it cascades in riverlets and becks.

'Oh, oh, oh,' I say, rocking him, rocking him. 'Oh, oh, oh.'

Meanwhile no doubt the rabbit man sings in the woods:

> *The moral of my story is,*
> *Weile, weile, wáile,*
> *Don't stick your penknife*
> *in your baby's back*
> *Down by the river Sáile.*

I am standing with Billy Kerr in the kitchen. The lamp must soon be lit but no one is thinking of lighting it. It is the day following. All the excitement of the trip to Baltinglass is over. The children are both asleep. The boy has chosen a teddy bear, which lies now at his side in the bed.

Something preoccupies Sarah. She is up

the top of the room in the shadows, at her habitual looming. Maybe it is a great relief that afflicts her, for it is like an affliction too, this escape from horror and danger.

'Maybe I should be off,' says Billy Kerr lightly.

Sarah doesn't answer him exactly. She passes from the shadows down a little closer to us.

'But why did you think that it might be Billy Kerr did take the little one?' says Sarah to me, as if the same Billy Kerr were a thousand miles distant.

'Because he said it, he said it to me, that if I interfered again, he would hurt a thing close to me, that's what he said . . .'

'Did you say that to her, Billy?' she says. Her voice is quiet, not gentle really, but quiet. 'Did you, Billy Kerr?'

'I never said such a thing, and I never would say such a thing,' says Billy Kerr.

'I'm telling you, I'm telling you, Sarah. I don't care now if you marry him in the morning. The boy is safe and I am only glad and grateful. But he said that to me, and I won't have him make a liar of me, no matter what.'

'The boy, as you say, is safe. Hah? All's well that ends well, hah?' says Billy Kerr.

'No,' says Sarah. 'All is not well. If you

321

said such a thing, and Annie for all her faults is not a liar, then Billy Kerr, you are part of the threats, part of the fear that afflicts me. I could not have you with me. I tell you, Billy Kerr, I could not have you with me, because I do have a sister's love for Annie, that I do, and I will not see her put under threats while I have breath in me.'

'So, grand,' says Billy Kerr. 'Because I said nothing of the kind.'

Sarah looks fierce at me. I have to shake my head. As a matter of fact in all honesty, I am weeping now, crying like a fool, because of Sarah's declaration. A sister's love. How house-high are those words.

'Look it, look it,' says Sarah, suddenly striding to the dresser and pulling out one of the two old books there. 'Look it, look it,' she says. 'Swear it here on this Bible that you never said that to Annie. Swear it here.'

'I don't want to be swearing on Bibles, Sarah,' says Billy Kerr helplessly.

'But you have to be, if ever you want me,' she says, with a kind of wild desperation all her own. 'Place your hand there, man, and swear you didn't.'

And he puts his right hand on it as bidden. There is a silence. I watch him, and I imagine I can hear his brain whirring like a lift of jackdaws. At length he draws his hand back abruptly.

'All right,' he says, 'I am an honest man. I cannot swear I didn't on the Bible, because, yes, I did say something like that . . .'

Sarah, weeping, places the old Bible on the table and passes across the flagstones of the kitchen and out the door.

'But I didn't mean a child, I didn't mean that child, or anything like it.'

But Sarah is gone.

'I meant the blasted hen, or suchlike,' he says, almost mournfully, to himself.

'It was you put the bucket on Red Dandy?'

'It was, Annie — because you wouldn't leave things alone! It was childish — indeed childish. But sometimes a man is.'

'Do you know,' I say. 'I almost admire you now, for that honesty. No, I do admire you. I don't suppose that is much use to you, my admiration.'

'Not much, Annie, not so much,' he says, and away he goes. I hear his nailed soles clip down along the yard and out the gate.

Fiercely I roam the offices of the yard and find her in the dairy, a strange choice considering it is my domain. But perhaps that has something to do with it. All is lined up, clean and scrubbed, the butter pats, the dishes, the counter with its star-bright tiles. Under the counter she is, like a sheep caught in an odd gap, like a sheep trying to escape the ravages of a dog. Her face and arms are forced tight into the corner, her back and rump dolefully sticking out, as if she hoped to disappear herself into the very wall, and be no more than a mouse or a spider. But Sarah takes up more room in the world than such as them.

'Sarah, dear, Sarah, dear,' I say.

'Go away, Annie, go away, go on away,' comes her muffled voice.

'Sarah, you cannot bore into the wall there. There is no hiding place there whatsoever.'

And I know she is weeping because her whole form is trembling like a moony tide against the harbour wall, shucking with sobs. Now she cannot help releasing the noise of those sobs, she sobs noisily into the wall. I reach under, and as soon as I touch her body she swings back to me, the great mass of elderly bones, the big horse face of her, the blinding eyes large behind the glasses, the hair that has taken whatever cobwebs were under the counter that I have missed in my cleaning. It shows therefore that the cleanest dairy can be criticized. I open my arms to her like an enormous child, and how gentle and soft she is, how warm, how damp her whole body from sorrow and tears. I must cradle her there, I must.

'The course of true love did never run smooth, did it, Annie!' she cries, all spit and misery. I pause at this. I am thinking of the truth of this in her particular case. There was never love. No one, it seems, spoke of love but her, in the private spaces between the houses of herself. But I must allow that gentle fiction, I must.

'That is truth, Sarah, and it was ever so.'

And I think of her again as a little girl, racing the sycamore seeds in the blowing lanes, telling the time from the clocks of the dandelions, swift and slight and really lovely, before the bits of her seemed to grow out just a few stops too far, and before the creep of age further grew out her nose, her heart, her silence. It was the quickness of her, the song, the promise. And it is hard for me to think it has all come to this, a huddled, cobwebbed woman in a country dairy, in my arms. And yet there is a moment later when I do not mind it, when somehow there is a moment of subtle change, when what she is and what she was combine, and I see there is something in Sarah that no one can gainsay, the unremarked quality of her courage, the beauty of her considerable soul.

'We will sell Billy the pony now,' she says, suddenly.

'We could keep him on if you wished,' I say.

'No, Annie. It is a new dispensation. If we are to have our fears, let it be so. We will sell Billy.'

As I am going in to bed later that night, I tidy away the famous book that made Billy Kerr tell the truth. I notice it is not in fact my father's Bible after all, but its twin, the complete works of William Shakespeare.

Things go back to normal. The world is strange. Billy Kerr returns to what he was, the working man of the Dunnes of Feddin. We fetch him up one Saturday to come and take Billy the pony away. But, by heavens, the pony is now so fat from our tending and his own inertia, he cannot fit back out through the byre door. With our permission, Billy Kerr demolishes the gable wall, and leads the pony out, and through the gate, Sarah and myself watching, and down the green road, and away to whoever is paying for him, we do not ask. Then Billy Kerr has two weeks of evening work, building the gable wall back up, course by course. He does not come into the house. He no more than raises a hand in greeting and farewell. Then the wound in the byre is closed, and he leaves us to our own devices. No buyer can be found for the trap, so it must moulder there, glorious, mildewed and doomed, in the lonely barn. There is a new load of bedding straw now fixed in there, offering a hundred new hiding places for the hens. Only Red Dandy wanders about, lost to herself, coming in the kitchen at every opportunity, mad as a march hare, and never again laying an egg that I know of. She is on our list now for the wringing of her neck, when chicken stew beckons. If Sarah can give up her pony, I can certainly give up my hen.

And so our peculiar and no doubt darkhearted planet runs ever further from the sun, the string of the days is tightening, the hours of daylight grow shorter, the summer is closing its shutters of gold and green for another year.

The swifts fly away, leaving their lodgings under the eaves. Matt flies away too, like the seasonal bird he is, or has become. Strange that he does not linger to see his own son, but then, I remember, there is that other life at the edge of the city, where he can meet all the sons he wants, in the company of his unknown Anna.

The summer is more truly over when he comes. We stand the children on the flag-stones of the kitchen. I am wondering what degree of an inch we have added to their sizes, with our stews and our milk and our eggs.

It is dark in the afternoon, there is more than a touch of autumn in the day, in the wind, in the darkening greens and browns of the land about.

In the corner of my eye, Sarah takes out some object from her cardigan, and kneels to the little girl. I am surprised by the sight. She leans forward and whispers something to her. The little girl nods sol-emnly and takes whatever it is, and places it in her own pink cardigan. I wonder what it might be. And later I ask Sarah, when they are gone, but she will not say. I ask the question and she shakes her head, nei-ther yes nor no, just shakes it, and says nothing. I realize then it must be something she cannot mention, or speak about, for fear of lessening its force. And then I am strangely happy for the girl, whether with good reason I do not know, and no doubt will never know.

Up comes his sharp little car before I have the thought and gumption to measure them at the wall. Never mind, it will do another time. I have taken their city coats out of mothballs and never a moth has been at them, but that they are like new, like the very first day of summer that they arrived. It is as if time had no degree, no width, no measure. All our joy of these children is spent and gone, and like the miser without money we have now nothing to hoard and count, and I feel it darkly. When he comes in with his long red beard and his green woollen suit, his brown tie the same colour as old heather, his yellow shirt, I am afflicted, just as I knew I would be, by the most grievous sorrow. But it is not my place to be sorrowful before this occasion. I smile and shake my nephew's elegant hand. He does not kiss me as of yore. Once he would run the length of the tiled path in Morehampton Terrace just to embrace me, gripping my lower legs with his little arms. Now he shakes my hand.

'Hello, chaps,' he says to the children.

'Hello, hello, hello, hello!' says his little son.

'Well,' he says, 'you have a proper Wicklow accent now,' and he laughs, as if a proper Wicklow accent might be a doubtful thing enough. I wonder how does the kitchen look to him, he so citified, so strange. Does he think it pitiably rural, plain and mean? The stains of dampness rising in the grimy walls must offend him. You cannot clean those stains, they are like the very stains of things that happen, no wily cloth will wipe them. The little boy is all delight, but the little girl not quite so much so. She is smiling but I recognise the signal of restraint, like a pony poorly broken faced with some rare task.

Their father stands foursquare now in the room, as present as a tiger. He seems so good, so strong, so young. But something passes across my mind, some shadow of the fate of this man's little sister Beatrice long ago, something to do with that, the guilt of it in him, the hurt unassuaged, and wedded to that, the oranges, the smell of oranges, the little boy kneeling at the shrine of his sister. That is a frightening thought. I know it is her hesitation has given rise to it. And is it a thought I should tell to him, to anyone? Is there some urgent message I should give? I do not know, the thought spins on the pool, spins and spins. Should I take him aside and tell him what I saw, at least, at least?

I am beginning to feel ill, actually ill. My stomach is cold and fiery at the same time. Could it still be possible, despite what Matt has said, that he is in effect a *culprit,* to use my father's word? The death of his sister, such a weight of guilty sorrow, has it done something to him, turned the course of the stream underground, so some necessary well in him is dry? He has suddenly all the aspect of a stranger, an interloper, a wolf. It is my task to protect her, she has been left in my care. Even in these last few moments, while she stands in the confines of this kitchen, she is my calf, my lamb. And who will protect her if Matt is wrong, and she is taken away from here? Assaulted, assaulted, said Maud in the bed, all those years ago. Assaulted, we echoed, assaulted! In my mind's eye I see again that wolfish man leap through the air on Kingstown pier.

She stands there, as if caught between two worlds. I feel some deep terror strike into my breast. My knees are sore with a kind of seeping poison. I feel old, wild, greatly at fault. I adore the boy, I adored him from the start. There is no great task in that. But she, she I have put in the second place of my affections. I know I have done that. Because she is a girl, but why, but why? Was I not myself a girl, one of three girls? Do I set so small a store on that? Why, why? I am staring at her. I could not describe the terror that I feel. I want to run out of the house and over hedges. It is as if I have never seen her before, never set eyes on her, proper eyes. Her mother is so strange, indifferent. She will never have the grace to help her. What am I to do? If I believed that Trevor had done anything to her, brought fear and hurt to her, what would I do? Wouldn't I have to kill him, to slay him with my hands, to prevent her being taken away by him? All her slim bones, her muscles, her slightness, her girlish knees, overwhelm me. I have been blind, evil, my mind is old and dark. I have not looked into her, seen her, cherished her, held her enough, talked to her, and now all my chance of rescue, her rescue and my own, is gone, is slipping away. If she has been violated then I must do a great thing, I must break out of all chains of love and family, of sense and ease, and become a thing of pure rage, like a bull coming in to cover, unbelievably strong and still as he was in ancient days, I must rise up and be another Annie, of impossible strength and motherly grace, and protect this girl, even if it must be by murder and destruction of all former days and loves.

Now the girl goes forward after all and hugs his knees.

It is such a relief, I almost cry out. Trevor looks over at me — perhaps I did make a noise — and smiles. Such a beneficent, graceful, charming smile. The girl has attached herself to his green trousers, her head down. But any fool can see the relief and ease in her little body. It is done so naturally, no one could suspect anything but that her hesitation was the normal reticence of a girl, a reticence born of love. It would be unnatural and hysterical to think anything else. Of this I am now certain. The boy was right, and Matt too — their father loves them. I cannot in honesty doubt it. I am so grateful to Matt for his sense, his knowledge. And the innocent knowledge of the boy! Thank God!

Now my old love for this man, when he was a little boy himself, returns like a blow. I am happy for him and miserable for myself! But should I still say something? No, I cannot. It might bring the boy into disrepute with his own father. *The least said the soonest mended. Let sleeping dogs lie.* I can almost hear my father's voice.

My thoughts are spinning now, spinning. Everything quickens in pace, like the gallop of a river in flood. Oh, he gathers them you might say clumsily in his arms and lifts them both bodily from the house. It is very strange. It is like the tinkers, like a theft of rope. Soon he sets them in the tidy car. All sensible thoughts flown from my head, I rush forth, my very clothes feeling like weights of lead, as if I am being fished at the bottom of the sea. I bang against the window glass at the rear of the car like a big, clumsy moth, I blow them kisses. But they are already in their new world, the world of their father. Soon they will be flown across the Irish sea in those silver aeroplanes, up in the sky like tubes of cigars. They will be torn from our tiny world, our miniature place, this yard in Kelsha without adornment. Will they remember anything of these days? Will they hold in their hearts the love I have for them, or will it all pass away like all the things of childhood? Will they ever understand my sorrow, oh maybe when they are grown themselves, here at the high gates of the mountains, where Keadeen breaks into the fiery bloom of heather, leaving all husbandry behind, and the Glen of Imail stretches wild and ruinous as a land laid waste by wars?

A cold, long siege, the winter coming, it will be, I expect. It is no wonder soldiers did not fight in that season, a fact to which my father often alluded, being almost a fighting man himself, without the weapons.

Well, there is no army quartered here, it is only myself and Sarah. But her presence will unknot the coming winds, and shake out the winter like a cloth both plain and rich.

We are like two spiders, in a dark corner of the world, things of no true importance, I am sure. But even the spider leaves a trace, a broken web blowing on the breeze. It does not need the notice of man. In its own manner it makes its simple statement, it writes its simple sentence and is gone.

It is the two of us here now, in Kelsha, myself and Sarah, as pensive as daffodils.

Someday, no doubt, all that we know will be gone, just as my father's world in its own time passed away, never to be savoured again. This Kelsha yard, henhouse, calf byre, hay barn, horse byre and milking shed, all will be levelled in the end. *Look on my works, ye Mighty, and despair,* said

Shelley for Ozymandias, on a broken stone in an empty land of dust.

Even the halves of songs I know, our way of talking, our very work and ways of work, will be forgotten. Now I understand it has always been so, a fact which seemed to heal my father's wound, and now my own. I think in the end he understood it too, and gained his salvation from that new courage he found, to go naked and unadorned into the next world. Even great kingdoms — Ireland, England herself — are subject to this law. How could this simple yard in Kelsha be exempt?

There is nothing in our lives that is important. Everything will be removed by that Great Fall.

But, although it will be winter soon, the wind of friendship will blow eternally from the south. And even after we have gone, something of that friendship will surely linger hereabouts. We will survive in the creak of a broken gate, the whistle of a bird, the perpetual folding and unfolding of the blossom of my crab-apple tree, a thousand little scraps of crinoline fiercely crushed and fiercely released.

Like the spider, although we will decay, something of us ever after will remain.